West of Love

D1293068

West of Love

A Story Cycle

by

Francis Davis

BRIGHT
HORSE
BOOKS

Copyright © 2017 by Francis Davis
All rights reserved.
Printed in the United States of America

Brighthorse Books
13202 N River Drive
Omaha, NE 68112
brighthorsebooks.com

ISBN: 978-1-944467-07-4

Cover Photo © iStock.com\lightkey
Author Photo: © Saul Mastandrea

For permission to reproduce selections from this book,
contact the editors at info@brighthorsebooks.com. For
information about Brighthorse Books and the Brighthorse
Prize, visit us on the web at brighthorsebooks.com.

For Sally, Tess, Max, and Sam

I don't want to repeat my innocence. I want the pleasure of losing it again.

—F. Scott Fitzgerald

CONTENTS

ACKNOWLEDGMENTS

"Glasnost" published in *Notes Magazine*; "Spring Break" published in *Third Wednesday*; "In The Kitchen" originally published as "Swallowing the Worm" in Ducts.org; "West Philly" published in *Story*; "Montana" published in *Atticus Review*; "Soft City Seattle" published in *Weber: The Contemporary West*; "Nowhere, Nebraska" published in *The Saint Ann's Review*; "Tokyo" published in *Apeiron Review*.

GLASNOST

FIRST, THERE WAS THE Russian with the blood-colored birth splotch dripping down his bald dome, all his funny talk, and then there was us, young and in love, living in that shitty apartment in West Philly across the street from The Red Sea, the Ethiopian place, where just last night, slender, elegant waiters had placed steaming platters of spicy lamb and vegetables before us, departing a moment later without a word. We'd eaten with our hands, a sweaty glass of beer at my side as we scooped up the meat with slices of flatbread. Perspiration poured from beneath my bushy locks, and you, sleek in thrift-store couture, smiled your cool blue Swedish smile.

This was 1989, the year the Berlin Wall came down, that looming menace of pending nuclear disaster finally flushed away, a threat replaced almost immediately by AIDS and the ridiculously trumped-up rhetoric leftover from Reagan's War on Drugs.

That morning, you were still in bed. It was November, a cold, blustery day, and we were thinking about heading to your mother's, but first I was out and about, rustling up some coffee and breakfast. You'd wanted to leave the city by then, but I'd convinced you to stay for one more year, selling it as safe because we lived close enough to Penn's campus, which was mostly true. But when Philly finally failed, we would move out to City Line Avenue before finding the house in Ardmore, the yellow Victorian where I thought we might just live forever. You moved out after three months.

This was before that.

We were still living in that skinny roach-infested apartment ten blocks from Penn. The bathroom and kitchen were small with nameless black grime between the tiles, but the front room had bay windows that let in the good light of the afternoon and fancy French doors that gave our place just a hint of the elegance we assumed our future held. Above us lived an old man with a mutt named Midnight, a dog he always called Girl. Each morning the man and his dog would shuffle up and down the stairs, and I can still hear his voice calling in my ear, "Get up there, Girl, get up there."

Indeed, a funny place for nirvana.

We were young enough that everything still held a tinge of wonder. Was the Chinese man who lived next door, and whose TV always glowed blue, a graduate student? An immigrant janitor? Someone's fool-hearted cousin? What was up with the older couple who lived below us? A couple we never saw but heard arguing all the time. Why were they even together? How did people get like that, so angry and disillusioned? You were working your computer job, reading Flaubert in the evenings and taking pottery classes on the weekends. I was still jobless six months after graduating, still dreaming about teaching in Japan or hitchhiking to California, and all the while, the empty tall boys I kept in Hefty bags behind our French doors kept accumulating. But the biggest mystery might have been the single guy on the first floor, the James Spader look-alike who every other Friday hosted an open mic poetry reading in his apartment. He let people shuffle in from the streets, homeless guys, a few anarchist punks from the boarded-up squat down the block, but mostly earnest poets clutching their notebooks, some even wearing berets. We went once, remember, to this Spader's reading, but he didn't even recognize us, and I turned small after I read because no one had recognized my budding genius.

A few blocks southwest—deeper into the scorched heart of West Philadelphia where my people, my parents and grandparents, had been born—lay a stretch of blocks where citizens regularly gunned down other citizens for all the usual dumb and drastic reasons. Four hundred and ninety-one murders in the city that year. You wanted to leave, but I told you it was safe when it was light, which was mostly true.

That morning, I was up early and headed to the deli, chasing a muffin, maybe a fat banana one with flakes of cranberry and carrots, and a jumbo takeout coffee for each of us—this, years before Starbucks, and eleven months since our Christmas gifts had been stolen from the back seat of your yellow VW Beetle. We'd gotten back from your mother's late that Christmas Eve and I'd said the gifts would be fine in the car until morning. When you discovered the shattered back window of the Beetle on Christmas morning, the gifts gone, you broke down in tears. Upstairs, after your weeping had died down, I tried to be funny for you, imagining some sad-sack thief opening up the Hickory Farm gift box of cheeses and sausages I'd purchased for my old man, but you just got angry then, angrier and angrier, thinking I was a fool for laughing at our hard luck. You were always so much more a warrior than me, fierce when it came to the city and your people.

"They probably had their reasons," I said that Christmas morning, getting stoned before we drove out to my father's place in Boothwyn.

"Reasons? Are you serious? Stewart, don't be stupid. What kind of person steals Christmas gifts?"

·

BUT ENOUGH. I WANT to talk about the morning I brought you the coffee and muffin, the morning the Wall came down. Outside, the bare branches of the spruces and oaks in front of our place shook in the wind so stepping inside with the steaming coffee, you waiting in the back bedroom, felt exactly like the epiphany it was. You lay in bed still, so lovely, sleepy but up, and I came to you quickly, putting down the hot coffee on the nightstand, a dime-sized slurp spilling over the cup's lip and burning the knuckle of my index finger.

"Shit."

"What?"

"Nothing. I burned myself."

"Here. Let me."

You kissed my burn and then my lips, giggling, saying my lips were cold. I whispered your name. We turned on the set because I'd heard something at the deli about the Soviet Union and Europe. No cable in those days, so we tuned to PBS and watched in jaw-dropping amazement as the Germans broke apart their wall with hammers, pickaxes, and their own bare hands. The bricks crumbled away to dust. People wept. People sang. We giggled. Russian guards and Germans shared flutes of champagne. One guard asked, "What have I been doing for the last twenty years?" David Hasselhoff even showed up. I had the lofty idea of taking you there in our bed, your mouth still holding the smoky taste of sleep, as the news of the dead wall filtered in from the TV. I wanted it to be like the famous photo of the sailor kissing the nurse at the end of WWII. I thought I'd always remember it, and I do, but it didn't go the way I'd imagined, little does, and I'd not yet gotten accustomed to that fact—how so little of life unfolds as planned.

Afterward, we stayed in bed and split the muffin as the radiator hissed and the images on the TV began to repeat themselves. Our talk turned to Dean and Sandy. Sandy was one of your seven sisters, Dean her boyfriend, just out of the Air Force, a skateboard-punk gone military. He didn't fit any of our stereotypes. Mostly, he was just an orphan with a smirk, the one your family kept—not me, the mixed Jew they threw back.

"Do you think it'll work out between Dean and Sandy?"

"Probably," I said. "Though I don't get Dean. He thinks he's like *James* Dean or someone, right?"

"It's his mouth."

"What?"

"My sister likes his mouth."

"His mouth? What's so special about his mouth?"

"It's wide and his lips curve nicely."

"What? What about my mouth?"

"It's a mouth," she said, smiling. "It's OK."

I looked at her and grinned, muffin between my teeth, goofy with love—a perfect moment.

And then it was gone.

"Look at this," I said. "This is some historic shit. They're breaking apart the wall."

"They're getting souvenirs, Stewart."

"But it's more than that."

"Yeah, now we won't have to worry about getting blown up anymore."

"That's something."

With those words the air left the room and we sat like some recently unearthed treasure that wasn't worth the trouble; our love like cement drying, and we both knew we were too young for this feeling. On the tube, they were already telling us a story—flashing back to Reagan speaking before the old wall: "Mr. Gorbachev, tear down this wall," shaping it into history.

What did we expect? It felt like my life, but you were right, I guess, because in less than two years we were done and chunks of the graffiti-stained wall got scattered across the globe—a few made it, years later, to eBay, and one even ended up behind a urinal in Las Vegas, a tourist trap, a place I'd visit on a lark during one of my last drunken road trips with Jill. But I don't want to talk about that. I want that morning back—before we spoke of Dean's mouth, before the noise of the background commentators—just the sun streaming through the bedroom window warming our fresh limbs and my fingers tracing your lips, the deli coffee still hot on the nightstand as your lips cooled my knuckle and I whispered your name.

SPRING BREAK

WE WERE THERE, TOGETHER, in the Poconos, at your
sister's house, the lucky one, Danielle, who'd married the
radiologist, Ron, the guy with the porn collection unhid-
den on his bedside bookshelf, as if a doctor didn't have to
bother to hide his porn like the rest of us. You and I were
playing the married couple, and it was wondrous up there
among all that gloomy quiet, not far from the Delaware
Water Gap with its virgin forests, mirrored ponds and the
ever-gushing Alleghany. Ron and Danielle were in Bar-
bados for the week, a trip I couldn't even begin to fathom,
and the big story in the *Pocono Record* was the deaths of
two kayakers who'd drowned when their fiberglass boats
flipped, trapping them beneath the rapids. I'd read you this
story over our Cheerios, the happy couple taking in some
sorry news over breakfast. We had the run of Danielle and
Ron's rambling house in the woods, and the charge of their
two beautiful towheaded children—Lacy and Ryan, ages
five and eight. During the week we'd carted the children to
restaurants, playgrounds, and supermarkets, and people in
the street had stopped to comment on their beauty—these
ghost children, our children, the echo of the children we
would never have, the little boy I'd wanted to call Blue, you
preferred Zoe for a girl. When was this—1989 or 1990? I
can't remember for sure, but by now these kids must be finished with college, maybe married, maybe with children of
their own. I don't know. I haven't heard from you in so long
that none of this seems real now. It doesn't seem real that
deep into my own marriage with children and a mortgage,

I can so easily imagine stepping back away from this life, toward you. Can you hear me, Rita, wherever you are? All these years later and what a ridiculous man I've become. It's no torch I'm carrying, just my own wrinkled blue heart.

We were young and happy in this house in the Poconos, so unlike our tiny apartment in West Philly. There were no roaches to battle, muggers to flee, parking spots to fight over. The air tasted of pine and fir, and with no other houses in sight, just the rolling hills and tree-shrouded valleys, we screwed outside on your sister's deck chairs, and maybe it was this time at your sister's that planted the seeds for my flight to Montana, my wanderings there, after you were finally gone.

That week in the woods, I'd pinched some weed from your brother-in-law, the mechanic, and on TV it was March Madness. Bo Kimble was shooting free throws with his left hand in memory of his dead buddy, Hank Gathers, who earlier that month had collapsed on a basketball court and died. Kimble didn't miss once. I'd gotten you all excited about that, talking up sports as a metaphor, as essentially a modern-day religion, and you believed me, even though, looking at it from another perspective, it's not that complicated, it's the same every single time— someone loses, someone wins. But back then you believed almost everything I said. You told me I taught you how to think, and I didn't quite know what to say to that. I haven't seen you in over twenty years, since that day I saw you in Anderson Hall by the elevators at Temple University and I realized you didn't love me anymore.

Once during this week at your sister's, you were out picking up some groceries and I was left to mind the kids. Lacy was upstairs napping, Ryan was in the backyard making a fort, searching for a treasure, killing insects.

"Keep an eye on him," you said. "Just make sure he doesn't get hurt."

"What could happen?" I said. "He's just a kid. We're in the Poconos. This is paradise."

"Stewart, seriously, he could do anything. He's a little perv too. Don't let him get into Ron's stuff."

"Baby, we're born perfect, you know. I'll just let him do his thing."

"Stewart. Stop."

"I know. I'll keep an eye on him."

Twenty minutes later I was slurping up some pasta, reading the *Daily News* when I turned around to see Ryan on the outer lip of the back porch railing skirting along there—a dangerous, dumb thing to do, something only an eight-year-old could dream up. I looked at him hard, told him to be careful. He smiled at me, continued his scoot, and I went back to my newspaper. I reasoned to do more could alarm him, could cause him to fall. Eventually, I knew he'd get bored and come back to the safe side of the porch.

Today, December in Nebraska, that spring is a ghost dancing in my memory as I sit in my basement office, rushing to record these distant voices as the footsteps of my children and wife pound the floorboards above my head like wild horses. I remember how in the Poconos we stripped and lay in the sun on your sister's deck, the air on our bodies like a miracle after a long winter indoors in the city. But you were shy even there, even then, and when a plane flew overhead, you covered your breasts with your arms and I took you upstairs and got you in bed. Your skin glistened white, and I squiggled down past your belly to kiss you between your legs the way you liked. You sucked in your breath, bringing your knees together, and asked me to stop when really, I knew, that was the last thing you wanted. You had told me once you didn't understand the waves fluttering along the bottom of your belly, didn't understand the way your thighs shook, when I did what I did with my tongue, so you brought your legs together that day, your thighs flush against my cheeks, gripping my face with your cunt, and begged me to stop. But I didn't. And I can still smell your musk, still taste your salt, still hear your voice pleading for me to stop—to please god stop, stop, stop, stop.

ROXBOROUGH

WE WERE DRUNK AT Turner's, all of us—except you, of course, who didn't drink there (or anywhere), but did teach gymnastics to middle schoolers three nights a week in the backroom of the tavern, this labor on top of your regular job as a computer programmer. Your brother Bill, a smarty like you, was behind the bar that night, six foot and lumbering, trimmed blonde beard, while Gabe and I were in front of it, drinking our Jameson, talking our shit. Bill slid me another whiskey, asking if I'd finished *Tin Drum*, the famous Holocaust book by the German writer that he'd loaned me a few months back. I hadn't yet cracked it, and never would, a fact I felt guilty about until years later when the author, who'd portrayed himself as a Jewish sympathizer, admitted he'd lied about his background and had actually been a member of the SS.

"Not yet," I told Bill that night at the bar. "One of these days I'll get to it."

He raised his eyebrows and moved down the bar toward someone barking his name. You always said Bill, the lone male among your eight siblings, was the most like you, and I'll never forget the befuddled look he gave me fifteen months later when I showed up at your family's annual picnic two weeks after you'd left me for another guy. It was like he was seeing me for the first time, the ghost you'd left. Your departure was like a sore on my tongue, something I'd rake my teeth over again and again—just to make sure it was still there, this soreness the only part of you I still had, the part of you that had gone.

But this was before that. Tonight at Turner's, I was twenty-three, king of the world. One of your crew asked Gabe and me if we wanted to play darts.

"Hell, yeah!" we roared, carrying our drinks to the board in the back. You were at a quiet table in the opposite corner conversing with one of your sisters, wearing your long tweed coat, your scarf unwrapped on the table, waiting for us to have wasted just enough time and drunk just enough alcohol to call it a night. Nelson Mandela had been released from prison in Cape Town that very same day, but no one other than Bill, or maybe you, would have been talking about that because way over in Tokyo, a place where I'd end up for a short time after you left me, the heavyweight champion of the world, Mike Tyson, had been slapped silly in the boxing ring by a journeyman fighter named Buster Douglas.

"Did you hear that Tyson lost?" one of the bar's cronies shouted to our little group by the dartboard.

I looked back at you, caught your eyes; you smiled.

Behind the bar, Jimmy *was* saying something about Mandela, and when I asked a guy with a mullet next to me who beat Tyson, he looked at me like I was the dumbest boy in Philadelphia.

"Just some other nigger," he said.

What I want to say is I was beautiful once, as were you, and nothing I write here can change that, not this, not Turners, not ugly talk among ignorant people. What I want to remember, but can't, in any real detail, is you and me at that other tavern on Chestnut Street, our place, away from these fools, how it was when we were alone, how we listened to each other's dreams. I wanted you soft in my hands; I wanted to protect you, and for a short time we loved one another like that, like only the young can—fiercely and freely, as if we were the first to feel this way. Now, I'm no longer young, nor beautiful, and you exist for me only in memory, in my shrunken young man's heart, encased in the leathery one I now carry.

"Who?" I asked mullet man, ignoring his slur.

He just shook his head and turned away, letting me know I'd failed some test of white manhood. Let me say, this was your neighborhood and these were your people. How they defined you and how you defined yourself against them was certainly part of what brought us together, but in the end it might also have been what finally drove us apart. My people fled West Philly in the 70s, while yours stayed in the northwest tip of the city, fighting it out, carving out a section there for their own kind. It takes a certain type of person to do so, I assume. Not me.

Someone finally said it was Douglas who had beaten Tyson, but I couldn't fathom this mystery man taking down the great champion. Tyson was at the peak of his powers, a warrior in the ring. He'd never lost a fight, but after that night he would never be the same again. I thought about my dad and brother, how at my dad's house, my brother would be in shock because he loved Tyson and watched all his fights with the old man.

"Who the fuck is Buster Douglas?" I asked Gabe.

"Throw your dart," Gabe said.

I couldn't get my head around it, but no one else seemed to care. Who knew that in a little more than a year I'd be in Tokyo myself, and less than six weeks after that I'd be back in Philadelphia living with another girl, not you? We would see each other shortly after I'd returned from Tokyo, at Temple University, where you had started taking French classes. I was there to get transcripts for graduate school or some such shit—already planning an escape that would take three long years. At the elevator where we bumped into each other, you looked shocked for only half a second.

"What are doing here?" you asked, wearing that same long tweed coat, the same wool scarf covering your slender neck.

"I came back," I began, but before I could explain, you laughed and shook your head, as if this were just one more example of why you'd left in the first place, which I suppose it was.

The elevator doors cracked open and you climbed in. I watched you punch the buttons, watched the doors slowly close. Everyone from that part of my life is gone now—you, Gabe, my father, my brother, that whole sad crowd. It was one reason I fled to Montana. I felt it all slipping apart, and I knew I had to go somewhere, anywhere but there watching you press the elevator's buttons, waiting for the doors to close with that look on your face, that smirk, as if I too were just one of the crowd—the loud, stupid crowd.

That rest of that night in the bar, I forget. It's lost with all the other nights, somewhere, but I'm guessing we went back to West Philly in your Accord and that on Monday I'd have gone to work, though I can't be sure, I can't remember, it might have been a month or so before I'd landed the job at the publishing company. Still, let's just say we went back to our place, ate boxed mac and cheese, talked some, made love. Let's say we were happy and quiet in each other's arms in our bed as we listened to the murmur of our neighbor's TV from below, waiting, without knowing we waited, for this story to be born.

LOVE PARK

I WAITED IN THE rain, slumped like a bum in my surplus army jacket beneath the polished-steel LOVE sculpture at 15th and JFK, the Replacements wailing through my Walkman: "No one to claim us, no one to name us," waited inside the patter of the rain against the red L-O piled like blocks atop a V and an E, waited in the murky light from City Hall looming across the street as shoes of office workers scurried past me and the wheels of cars and buses splashed through the water on the street. In my canvas satchel, maybe Kerouac, my Svengali whispering in my ear that my heart belonged not here, but on the road away from Rita, lovely Rita. Earlier that evening, at the Full Moon, I'd wanted to kiss a stripper's fleshy pussy, the one with the dyed blue pubic hair, wanted to put her in my mouth, her raisin clit, and suck her like a jewel, and if not her, maybe Rita, that night, when we got home, out of these wet clothes and into bed.

When Rita finally did pull up in her Accord, beeping once, twice, three times, I'd leapt up like a dog, still hard in my pants, and jogged over awkwardly before I opened the door and slid in, dissolving into the lovely warmth of that car.

"Rita, my love," I said, leaning toward her. "Let's go home and new pleasures prove."

She smirked, waved her hand, maybe weary of my English-major ways, and pushed the buttons on her cassette deck, saying, "Oh, Stewart, just shut the door. You're all wet and I'm tired."

•

BUT THIS STORY WAS a few years after that. Ted and I were enjoying one of our last epic binges, a ridiculous rite leftover from our time together at Temple. We'd settled in like kings at an old-man bar in the Northeast, already having drunk up the afternoon and most of the evening at Dirty Frank's, where we had split $3 pitchers of Rolling Rock among our fellow art students, freaks, and drunks, trying to talk it all out. Every last word.

Earlier that morning hustling home from the el, I'd glimpsed two men in the street tussling over a gun, a tiny pistol. My mouth had felt cottony from the previous night's beers, my heart grinding away at the clutch of failure beginning to cling to my bones, and the tangled flash of silver hit me like a transmission from another universe, another life. It looked not unlike the hand-printed sign perched on the dash of the 1970 Volkswagen Bus down the block from my apartment, *$500 or best offer.* I wanted to buy the VW and cruise to San Francisco, but every time I bought up the possibility to Rita she'd simply shrug and ask, "And what would we do once we got there, Stewart?" Rita, loveliness aside, just didn't get it. Didn't understand the desire to burn through your life just because you could.

I was trying to tell Ted how the flash of the gun was an electrified moment, a TV moment. It had raised the hairs on the back of my neck and infused my cotton mouth with the metallic taste of dread, yet I hadn't even broken stride, hadn't really even given it another thought until just now, talking about it in this old-man bar.

"You mean, dear Stewart, your feelings have calcified? The deep blue sin of urban existence has sucked out your empathy like venom from a bite."

"So empathy is the poison?"

"And language is a virus."

"Fuck that. Burroughs is too cynical."

"Does that make it less true?"

I shrugged, sipped at my beer.

"OK. Here's a question—what exactly did you think the moment you saw the gun? What were the words in your head?"

"Ted will like this story," I said. "I thought, here is a story for Ted."

"Exactly, my brother. Exactly."

He brought a shot glass of Jameson to his lips and drained it with dainty precision.

You see, Ted, along with immense quantities of cheap beer and quality whiskey, swallowed stories whole. He was a huge man, well over three hundred pounds, brilliantly sarcastic—a drunk and a fool, my best friend. By this time, he'd already burned through at least two lives, dropping out of high school to become a truck driver only later to earn his GED and a B.A. before heading to Chicago on a full-ride scholarship to Loyola. He'd fled Loyola just a few months ago, returning to Philly defeated but proud, telling me how during his very first departmental meeting, as the other new grad students took turns introducing themselves as Marxists, Feminists, Historicists and Post-Structuralists, Ted had smirked, thrown back his shoulders, and announced, "Ted Jenson, Gemini." The room had looked at him with open mouths and furrowed brows, not a smile in the crowd.

Now, we joked in our typical college-boy fashion about the cheap wood paneling, the bad art hung there, the sad songs on the juke box. The bar sat in Kensington, just a few blocks from Ted's house, the same section of Philly where Gary Heidnik, horrible Gary Heidnik, had done his awful deeds. You might remember Heidnik. If not, Google him.

Read up on how this psychopath had boiled the head of one of his victims on his kitchen stove while he kept five other women chained in a pit in his basement until one of them had finally escaped and brought back help. Heidnik was caught in 1987. This was late 1989 or early 90, so his story was still in the air around those parts, but what's particularly important to this story, as well as creepy as hell, was a new psycho killer was on the loose picking up prostitutes from seedy bars and murdering them in alleys and parking lots—a killer, by the way, who was never found. And if I'm going to be absolutely honest here, I need to tell you that Ted had a troubling fascination with serial killers—and that all the victims of this latest spree had come from the Northeast. And the last woman had been last seen alive at the very bar where Ted and I now sat.

Ted was telling me this as he ate bar pretzels—a way too weird smile on his face.

"I mean, the killer could be here right now," he said, his beard catching salt crumbs.

And if I always had a Kerouac or Ginsberg stuffed in my backpack, Ted always had at least one biography of a serial killer slipped in among his books, but it was not until that very moment, as he told me the story of the killer on the loose, that it hit me that Ted fit the profile of a serial killer perfectly—highly intelligent with the ability to look at life abstractly, to pathologically distance oneself from one's emotions—a profile I'd learned from Ted, by the way.

"C'mon, Ted, cut the shit. That's just too weird."

"I'm just saying it's possible, Stewart. Either he's been here or he hasn't. The cat in the box is either dead or alive, but if you don't look into the box it's both, right? Dead and alive?"

"Just like those women in the basement?"

"What?"

"Nothing," I said. "You know your bullshit. The whole point of that riddle is something can't be both dead or alive. No one needs to see something happen for it to have happened. Or are you suggesting we check the bar for fingerprints?"

Ted shrugged as the waiter placed a platter of shriveled up chicken wings before us. The tavern was just your average dive bar with booths carved from the back wall, a four-sided faux-mahogany bar in the middle of the floor—an island marooned in the middle of the Pacific. It was situated under the el tracks, so it shook gently every fifteen minutes or so from a train passing overhead as if someone were trying to wake you from a nap. Ted picked up one of the wings and motioned to the surly-looking guy in a Flyers cap on my left, saying, "I'm just saying the guy could be sitting next to you right now. He could be in here right now."

Ted loved this meta-moment crap, and I must say, I miss those days, burning away my youth with ridiculous stories and drink—we were right there in the middle of it, living a story we were telling ourselves and we were happy, sort of, but before I could say another word, the guy Ted had motioned to asked me in a gruff voice, "Are you Jewish? You're a Jew, right?"

"What's that?" I asked, turning to him with a Howdy Doody smile pasted on my face, more shocked than anything, shocked I could feel shocked even though I was quite drunk. This was a first, this Jew business. Ted started laughing like the maniac he surely was.

"What's your name?" the guy asked. He had greasy red hair spilling out from under his cap and was missing half of one of his front teeth.

"Stewart."

"Stewart what?"

Ted elbowed me in the ribs—shot glasses, dirty ash-trays, and packs of cigarettes were littered across the face of the bar.

"Stewart Simmons?" I said.

"Jesus, what kind of name is that? That's a Jew name. Fucking Simmons. That's the fucking Sabbath or some shit you celebrate, right? Look at your nose. You're a Jew? Don't you know this is an Irish bar. IRA. Goddamn Jews are everywhere. Did you hear me? An Irish bar. I-R-A." He tapped the bar with his index finger as he said each of the letters just in case I didn't get his point.

Ironically, years later, my father would reveal that indeed I *was* Jewish. And even though, by that time, I'd already heard the story from my cousin, I acted surprised. I had to. Dad was in Missoula to see my new baby daughter and we were eating at a diner. This was about a year before he died, and when he told me the secret of my Jewish roots the night I'm describing here came back at me like a rock from a slingshot.

"See, your pop-pop was Jewish," Dad said. "When he married my mother, he converted, and his people cut him off. They hated Catholics. That's how people were back then. They wouldn't have anything to do with him, Dad's family, so we did the same to them. We never worried about them. We forgot about them."

Dad waved his hand out in front of him as if he were chasing flies from his cheesesteak.

"I'm not Jewish," I told the guy next to me in the bar.

"Yeah, sure you're not. You're a fucking Jew."

"I'm not a Jew."

"You don't even know," he said.

After that, after a few more shots, Ted and I played

one last game, calling out names we wished were our own. Dead-drunk by now, fools, children, we were just jabbering nonsense, and I do wonder if, beneath all of this, Ted ever really did hurt anyone.

"Jack, Julius, Hank, Max," I said

"David, Sting, Hector, Augustus," Ted sang back at me.

For a while then, I called Ted Gus and he called me Jack. We thought all this hilarious and were very close to the part of the evening when Ted would wrap me in a bear hug and tell me he loved me—but we weren't there yet. We still had to walk to his house where I would crash for the night, walk through streets that were OK, sort of, if you were white, but not so safe if you were anything but.

"Luke, Joel, Cameron," Ted said.

"Howard, Wyatt, Ted," I rasped

He looked at me, his eyes jumpy and red.

"I didn't know you cared, Ted," he said, his voice a falsetto.

"I don't, Dick," I said. "Dick, I don't care about you at all."

YEARS LATER, AFTER I'D left Philly for Montana and then Montana for Nebraska, Ted would tell me over the phone how in the days we were students together, he was in the habit of getting blasted and driving around North Philly until he found a prostitute on a corner willing to climb into his car and blow him for twenty bucks as he circled around in his mother's beater Chevy, high on coke, the car stereo blasting Neil Young or Lynyrd Skynyrd. Not a good story, but a true one. He told me all this as his first wife was in the midst of leaving him. He said he'd always asked the prostitute their names, as if this excused anything, but I imagined the random, illicit thrill of it, not what resulted from it, not how when he married his wife she made him get an HIV test, nor how after she'd found Jesus (some more) and was deciding to leave him, Ted was left with the sad choice of going Christian or losing his woman. I thought only of the moment, driving around high on coke, a stranger's mouth warm on your dick.

"I could do Chesterton's Christianity, the thinking man's Christianity," he would say over the phone that day.

Ted was drunk, of course, he only called after he had been drinking for hours, and I didn't bother reminding him that he didn't believe in God because, really, I wasn't sure if he did. Either way, it hardly mattered—those weren't our questions. Ted just wanted his woman to love him again, and as he rambled on about Chesterton, another story sprang to mind—how in the years between dropping out of high school and earning his GED, Ted was fooling with a deer rifle in his room, cleaning it or some such shit, when he told me the gun had gone off and the cops had come and he'd sheepishly explained what had happened, showing the police the bullet hole in his bedroom wall, apologizing. I never believed that story, not entirely, and still think Ted was doing more than just cleaning his rifle.

What I've always suspected about Ted was that he, like me, like most people, just didn't have the guts to tell the truth. Or more precisely, he had stories that didn't fit with what people thought about him when they thought about him. We all have these stories, but most people keep them to themselves. I wish Ted were here now because I might ask him what does *not* telling a story do to it? Does it become like that cat in the box? Both dead and alive. Maybe that thought experiment wasn't complete bullshit.

After we left that bar that evening, after we returned to Ted's house, and he cooked me an egg and cheese sandwich, I tried to talk a bit about how I felt my life was beginning to slip away from me, how I didn't really want a job in publishing, though Rita thought that was a fine idea.

"It can't just be this—can it?" I asked.

"What can't?"

"Us. This. I mean sometimes I look at Rita and I can't fathom another day, but at the same time I know she's the one. I know this."

"One. Two. Zero. One. Binary thinking, my friend, is the problem," Ted said. "You have to read Wittgenstein."

"OK. Tomorrow."

"And tomorrow."

"A dusty fucking death."

"I love you, man," he said, getting up to hug me.

Ted lived with his mother, grandmother, and two or three uncles, one of whom was more than a little crazy and roamed the attic late at night, muttering about rice paddies, trip wires, and the ghostly fierceness of Ho Chi Minh. He had suffered unknown calamities in Vietnam, this uncle, wounds we couldn't even begin to fathom. That night, our hug done, we heard something drop on the floor upstairs, and Ted and I glanced up at the ceiling.

"What's wrong with him?" I asked Ted.

"Too much of life," Ted mumbled, sitting back down at the table.

"What do you mean? Nam?"

"I mean his story is over."

I began to say something else, but Ted cut me off.

"Forget about it, Stewart. Just finish your eggs."

We settled into our meals, enjoying the egg and cheese sandwiches, content in the moment, knowing nothing of what waited for us, how I'd drift away to Montana after Rita left, while Ted would find his Jamaican bride, and then, after a few unmoored years, his Irish one.

Years after this night, Ted sent me an email, hinting at the curve his story had taken. He wrote in his email that he had some big news, but he wanted to give it to me over the phone. *It's going to blow your mind, Stewart,* he wrote. What he told me when he finally called was that he'd found his Irish lass (they had been Pen Pals years ago and reconnected after Ted, drunk as a skunk, phoned her randomly one night—he could always talk, Ted), and after this first phone call, they'd agreed to meet for a weekend in New York—and after that trip went well, she'd asked him to move to Ireland and be her love.

"It's like that Donne poem," I said over the phone after I had received his email.

"Which one?"

"Forget it. It doesn't matter."

However, this story ends before that conversation. It ends with me staring at Ted's email: *It's going to blow your mind, Stewart* as my memory flashed to the LOVE statue, the dripping rain, that stripper's pussy, the men tussling over the pistol, the drunk accusing me of being a Jew, Dad telling me I was a Jew, Ted giggling over the lip of his shot glass, his uncle shuffling around in the attic. I thought Ted was finally going to fess up about his sadistic alter ego, finally going to tell the truth. He was going to tell where he'd buried all the bodies—every last one.

IN THE KITCHEN

As usual Rita waited in the car, while I was upstairs talking to an arty redhead in a cramped hallway of a Center City apartment, swallowing the worm. My new friend wore paint-splattered jeans, and a splotch of cobalt blue on her neck might have been a birthmark or a bruise, or just more paint. This was in Philly, years ago, and when I think of those times, I think of the talking that we did, all the talking, talking and talking at parties in long hallways crammed with people, bodies squeezing past bodies, distended, limbs contorted, bodies leaning, sitting, smoking, drinking, everyone's mouth open and hungry, like one of those horrible Hieronymus Bosch paintings.

But tonight, in this hallway, it's just the redhead and me. She's a girl whose name I will never know. We met just a few minutes ago in the kitchen, huddled by the stove, looking more, I'm sure, like characters escaped from an Edward Hopper painting, glad to be close, glad to be talking. Just two minutes ago, a guy in a leather jacket—a genuine leather jacket, this before every leather jacket was simply a reference to a previous leather jacket seen in a commercial, film, or Gap ad—had come huffing up the stairs, smoking, and asked, "Are you Stewart?"

When I nodded, he went on, "There's a blonde in an Accord parked out front and she asked me to tell Stewart to hurry up down."

Hurry up down, I thought.

What I didn't know at the time was that Rita's soon-to-be lover lived just two blocks away from where she sat in the idling car, but that's another story, and what I was wishing, while I stood there with the redhead, was that I hadn't called Rita to pick me up just moments before Ray Beckett had stepped into the kitchen and pulled a bottle of mezcal from under his trench coat like a rabbit from a hat. The bottle had a dead worm floating along its bottom, and Ray, enamored by this fact, had clamored on about it, telling us how it worked as an aphrodisiac, how the Aztecs used it to communicate with the gods.

AT THE TIME, RITA and I lived together in an apartment in Ardmore, out on the Main Line. We were free of the city, finally—or so we told ourselves. But I had no car, and I'd never wanted to leave the city. It was Rita who'd wanted to flee the city, wanting nothing more to do with the crime-ridden neighborhood surrounding the University of Pennsylvania where we'd lived for the last three years while I finishing my B.A. at Temple. I'd agreed to the move after Rita had agreed she would pick me up in the city on those nights I was still there after all the parties had ended, or the bars had closed, and the trains had stopped running. This was one of those nights, late Saturday, and I thought that gave me a certain prerogative, but mostly I just missed the strangeness of the city, our life there, the nights watching TV in our underwear, knee-deep into a sixer of Lowenbrau while eating take-out Ethiopian from The Red Sea across the street. Often, watching the local news at night we'd see yellow crime tape in front of a storefront window, a familiar window, we'd think, before the subtitle on the tube announced *Murder in West Philly* and we'd realize the familiar window was from the deli two blocks down, so close to where we lay our heads each night, so close to where we, under the covers, traced each other's young bodies, feeling at our luck and laughing at the fact that we had found each other so easily and at such a ridiculously tender age.

There were 491 murders in the city the year before we moved. The same story over and over: The owner of a store pulls out a sawed-off shotgun and murders two black teenagers he has mistakenly identified as thieves or two black teenagers murder a Korean clerk for sixteen one dollar bills. Each night before the news, I skipped across Walnut Street to The Red Sea and bought a take-out six-pack, seeking my relief.

So we moved to Ardmore. Made the deal. Now, she was below waiting. I had called from the kitchen phone well over an hour ago, in a lonely moment, a dead moment, when the party was at a lull, a moment before Beckett walked through the door and pulled out that mezcal bottle from inside his trench coat like a street-corner magician. It was just about then when I spotted the redhead looking at Beckett with the same bemused smile that was pasted on my face.

We had been talking in the kitchen, which overlooked the street, when I first heard the faint echo of a car horn.

Rita?

When the horn sounded again there was no doubt it was her, so I took the redhead's hand and guided her to the hallway. This was before Nirvana, before cell phones. Michael Stipe still had hair. No one but us knew of Morrissey, the Meat Puppets, Bad Brains. I was twenty-four. How cocky were you when you were twenty-four?

Then the guy in the leather jacket came in and told us about the blonde in the Accord.

"Is that your girlfriend?" the redhead asked, god bless her, this child, this girl, this young woman, this ruby princess, wherever she may be. I imagine her in Denver, a yoga instructor, sipping tea, finding her chi.

Once at a party just like this one in yet another hallway near another door, I had told a girl I couldn't go home with her because Rita, my Rita, was waiting for me at home. Waiting once again. Why Rita was always at home waiting is a mystery this story can't solve. She just was. She didn't drink; she didn't fool around, she was so serious and beautiful with imperial blue eyes. She wasn't interested in the foolishness that drew me in, but her body was liquid in my hands, her soft breasts and lovely puss were like epiphanies. I loved to lick and suck her, driving her crazy. She used to pull her legs together and beg me to stop. A virgin when I met her, a girlfriend of hers had to explain those waves she felt in her belly were an orgasm. This other girl at this other party, call her Heather, stroked my face when I told her about Rita waiting at home. She called Rita a lucky girl. I remember Heather well; her red lipstick and black hair. Her thick wool sweater couldn't hide the wonderful swell of her breasts. She wore a denim skirt and black nylon tights. She was young and pretty and she wanted me, offering herself for one night, but when I said, "No, I can't," all she said was Rita was a lucky girl.

She didn't know the story, didn't know that I had already fucked someone else, only to come home and fuck Rita, two girls within an hour of each other, both young and beautiful. I thought I was God. I was an asshole, yes, but still, after Rita did eventually leave me, do you know how many times I've thought of Heather? (To say nothing of Rita.) Can I say this? Can I explain how much all of this means? And it's not the pleasure, it's not the sweet pain, it's the possibility, this glimpse into another world where a guy like me might be seen pointing back, guffawing; beautiful women everywhere. I think I was beautiful once. I think everyone has moments. And I think our alternative selves race alongside us, mocking our choices. It's a 100-yard dash to the finish and we don't look left or right for fear of falling farther and farther behind what we might become.

That night in the hallway with the redhead, I told her, yes, that indeed it was my girlfriend waiting below.

"I'd be pissed if someone kept me waiting that long," she said.

It wasn't that simple, I explained. I told her about the promise, the deal brokered, and she asked me what I was given Rita in return for her taxi service, and I laughed and said, "My undying love, of course—to the end of my days," or some such asinine comment. I didn't know what mattered. I didn't know whom I loved. That night in the kitchen, I think I even put a hand over my heart. I was such a fool, but really there are millions of guys out there like me, telling the same jokes, living that same life over and over again. Everyone wants to be _____. (Rita, my love, had cheekbones carved from stone, a father who left her at thirteen, and seven sisters who backed me into a kitchen corner the first night I met them, demanding to know my intentions for their sister. I laughed them off and told them Rita's opinion was the only one that mattered. I was right. They believed me. One of the sisters called me "The Poet" from that night on. Another, Sandra, who dared me one night to drop a towel and jump naked into a pool, a dare I refused fearing that my dick would appear too small in the lamp light reflecting off the pool's purple surface, once told me me, "My sister never forgave my father for leaving. She doesn't forgive.")

I know this now. I understand.

"What do you do?" my new friend asked. The way I

remember it she had impossible green wolf eyes, this before colored contact lens, before fake boobs, before instant replay in football, before organic food. AIDS still a death sentence. The world just about ready for Kurt Cobain, but really, I thank god there were no cell phones that night because certainly Rita simply would have called mine. I might have answered, and the vibe of this conversation would have been broken, stopped short, this whole story sucked down and away into some smirking tech-savvy black hole. I would have been in the car on my way home by now, and possibly none of this would have happened. Rita wouldn't have been still waiting in the car, waiting and fuming, plotting her departure from my life, our life. Who knew? Not me. I smirked and answered my new friend.

"I'm a writer," I said, "I'm trying to write about my generation."

"What generation? We don't have a generation."

"Exactly. That's exactly it. Those bastards from the 60s stole it all away. Stole everything. We're still living in the freaking shadow of the hippies and how lame is that? That's the thing, that's what I want to write about."

"But no one believes all that crap. Peace, love and understanding? I mean be real. Those things don't even matter anymore."

"Yeah. No, that's what I'm saying, exactly, but I think the hippy aesthetic is coming back. There's going to be another Woodstock. I can feel it."

"Another Woodstock? Are you serious?"

We were on the verge of the great ironic age, a time when it would become impossible to simply state how you feel, to say, "I love you," or "What's wrong?" or "I'm scared," or "Help me." Those words are all gone now, but that night they lingered in the air, mixing with the cigarette smoke, the patchouli.

Speaking of irony: A month after this night Rita would leave me waiting alone all night in that apartment in Ardmore until the morning when she rushed in eyes wide with heat, telling me she was moving out. I would learn later that the man she left me for had an apartment at 19th and Chestnut, and in all likelihood she had already started it up with this guy (at least on a flirtatious level), and, I'm sure, while she waited for me she must have debated to herself the merits of leaving right then, at the peak moment of my ridiculous power, and to drive those two blocks, park her car (and why she never simply parked the Accord and came up and got me from the party is the second mystery this story can't solve) and buzz her new man.

Now, another guy, not in a leather jacket, came up and told me the same story about the angry young woman in the Accord.

"Don't know her," I said.

Smirk.

"You're bad," my new friend said.

We moved closer. We kissed, our one smoky kiss, before I would leave her forever, this girl leading me nowhere but to the next chapter of my life, allowing this part of my own little story to unfold as Rita sat below waiting, deciding our fate. And this is the truth because this is what she told me, what Rita told me that morning she came home and said she was leaving me for a man named Vijay.

"You fucker, I knew I was going to do this the night you made me wait on Chestnut Street for an hour."

"Forty-five minutes," I corrected her.

She said this. I said that. It's the truth. This really happened.

And I really did go then, after the kiss, I went back to the kitchen, the window there, opened it and leaned out like I was watching a parade, leaned out to give Rita a signal, to buy myself just a bit more time—just five more minutes, maybe one more kiss.

But she was already gone.

WAWA

I WANT TO TELL you about a certain Sunday morning in
the city of Brotherly Love, but before that I need to tell
you about Rita, lovely Rita, and the time she had stopped
her sky-blue Accord in the middle of a dark street in a bad
neighborhood and told me to get out. Get the fuck out.
We were somewhere between West Philly and the softer
confines of City Line Avenue, where Rita and I had lived
for the last six months in a one-bedroom apartment after
fleeing the chaos of the city. As usual, I was drunk and
Rita was angry—and it was late. I'd been an ass by lingering inside a bar as she waited outside in the car, and
then I'd badgered her on the drive back to our apartment,
pepper-spraying her with sarcasm. See, I hadn't wanted to
move from the city in the first place. I had no car and I'd
liked to carouse in the city with my boys, but Rita wanted
out, so we'd made the deal—we'd move to City Line and
she'd pick me up when I needed to be picked up. Now, here
she was telling me to get out of the car. Outside, the pave-
ment was crumbling, the houses looked abandoned, and
the city's coffin-gray light smothered the stars. Last year,
some four hundred Philadelphians had been murdered by
their fellow citizens. At first I was sure she was joking.

"What? C'mon, Rita, this is stupid. I'll shut up. I don't
even know where I am."

"Get out of the car!"

"Rita?"

"Get the fuck out of the car. Now."

I got out of the car, and it sped away while I watched,

stupidly, as if suspended between time, sure that she'd come back even as her taillights disappeared around a corner and the hum of her Accord merged into the murmur of the purple night.

"Rita? Fuck. Rita, what are you doing?" I whispered.

Before speeding off, she'd pointed the direction home, our home, but I took a wrong turn and found myself deeper into the bowels of West Philly, not far from where my grandparents and parents had been born and where I was raised for five years until our family had fled to the suburbs. Right away, I knew this wasn't good, and it only got worse when, from the blue, a man jogged up and shoved what looked to be a stick in a paper bag under my chin, asking for my wallet.

BEFORE THE ACCORD, RITA had driven her Bug, a yellow Volkswagen Beetle, and the very first time I saw her, she was stepping free of it, the cotton of her white skirt clutching her shapely thighs as she walked up the short hill to where I sat outside, on a lawn chair, slightly stoned from some weed I'd pilfered from my roommates stash. I was reading *The World According to Garp*. "Just Like Heaven" leaking from my stereo's speakers, Robert Smith's eerie moan that still does something to my stomach when I hear it today.

"Do you like The Cure?" she'd asked, smiling.

"The Cure? Yeah, I love The Cure."

And I did. It was true, and later that night this beautiful girl from Roxborough, a scratch of blocks on the outskirts of Philly, home to a stubborn group of working-class whites, like my people in some ways, had fallen in love with me, ridiculous me. These days I have to pinch myself, reminding the writer in me that this boy named Stewart, this character, will bleed if you cut him, will weep when his father dies, and would walk over crushed glass for a chance at the transcendent. And what is wrong with that, dear people? Is there anything wrong with wanting a god long after you have given up such belief?

That first night I'd met Rita, I held an orange in my hand, rolling it with my fingers as I made some kind of sappy speech to woo her. We were at a party. My room-mates had returned from the beach and brought with them girls from down the way, many girls, laughing girls, silly girls. Rita and I, on the other hand, were serious, so serious we found a serious corner and were talking seriously, each maybe sensing that the other would unlock our life, that the long scroll of paper that drops free from the sky and says you are this and this, but not that or that, would make itself known that very night. At the party, I picked at the orange, peeling it a bit, and said, "I wish you were this orange," perhaps one of the dopiest, most obvious things I'd had ever uttered. But she bought it. She allowed it. Rita, lovely Rita smiled, laughed even, having somehow already decided something about me. Maybe I could have said anything and she would have laughed and fallen closer, but I said the stuff about the orange and sensed that I'd won my life—somehow, I'd claimed a little bit of my future.

She could have said, "That is so corny."

Or

"You kind of creep me out."

Or

"Poet Boy, you are not the man that I'll finally let unbuckle my jeans."

She said none of these things. I don't think. The truth is I can't recall what she said. In fact, I can hardly recall any of our conversations, which must number in the thousands—a sad fact as facts go. In fact, I don't remember much about our life together, the details of our 1,465 days. I mean, I know all these things still live somewhere in my body—her smell, her lips on my neck, her crooked smile, her toughness—but the actual stuff we did together, the to-ing and fro-ing, the meals and the bills, the parties and the smiles, they are all mostly gone. What I remember was how she hovered over me when we loved. I do remember the weight of her in my hands, her feel when I slipped inside, how she pressed her thighs tight against my ears when I dipped down there, between her legs, with my tongue, her musky taste still in me. (Now, writing this, I do remember how once, visiting my father, Rita and I took a walk to a field where I played as a boy, and we tossed a football back-and-forth, this tossing perhaps the happiest moment of my life, and I like to think of that ball still somewhere in the air, midway between us—her giggles as high as my heart, her mouth wide open with delight.)

But what happened that night in the streets of West Philly was after all of that. It was after I'd cheated on her, after I'd stayed out late and fucked a snobby rich girl from my Romantic Poetry class (and I remember thinking that was ironic), and I did this more than once, and once even came home and fucked Rita the very same night, as if my life were some kind of movie. I guess you could say I was young, but what I really thought was the world owed me such pleasure. It was mine to take. After this happened, and before she left me for good, I'd asked Rita for forgiveness. We stood at the foot of the stairs in her mother's house during yet another party there—either a graduation or a holiday—and I stroked her cheek, touched her slender throat with the tips of my fingers and told her I was sorry. She cried some, but said it was OK, and I thought it was,

until the end, until she told me, laconically, she never forgave me, not really.

Now, we haven't spoken in years.

The last time she saw me she laughed. I was back from
an aborted trip to Japan, where I'd planned to teach English
for a year but had fled in less than a month.

"Why am I not surprised?" she had said when we'd met
randomly at the elevators at Temple, and I knew at that
moment she no longer loved me.

"Is that a rhetorical question?" I asked rhetorically.

I don't think I'll ever love someone the way I loved
Rita—completely and without pause, but what I should be
talking about are the cars—the Beetle versus the Accord.
She loved the Beetle, its bubble-shaped body, its eccentric, yet precise, German engineering with the engine in
the back, an engine whose oil she knew how to change—
one of the first facts she told me about herself. We fell in
love in that car, and she drove it until it died and then she
bought the Accord. The Accord never seemed to like me.
Long before she told me to get out of it that night in West
Philly, I sensed something bad lurking within it. My first
clue was when I drove it home to see the old man, without
Rita, and backed it into the neighbor's car, just a fender
bender, but when I explained what happened to my father,
something in his eyes said the very thing Rita's said that
day in the lobby, "You are tagged for something I want no
part of." I've always felt that way, selected, in both good
ways and bad, and I fear one day this might get me killed.
Once, while walking home from a keg party at a fraternity
house with a friend of mine, a kid walked up to me and
slugged me across the face. In the Bahamas, where I was in
a stall snorting a line of coke, a police officer kicked open
the door and his underling punched me flush on the jaw.

It stung for a week. Another man once threw a full stein of beer at my head after I referred to him as a jitbag, a term whose exact meaning I'd never considered until that very moment, Heineken dripping from my chin. And these are just some of the insults I weathered. I expect more. Many more.

But more than this West Philly drop-off, which I managed to survive, it's a certain Sunday morning I'm trying to get at here, one morning distinguished by its heat and the fact that Rita was gone. That Sunday, I rose from a friend's couch, where I'd crashed the night before, drenched in sweat, and slunk from his apartment feeling sticky and hung-over, badly in need of coffee. It was about 6:00 a.m., and I was half on the prowl for a Wawa and half just on the prowl. I found a Wawa, got my coffee, black, and stepped from the store, sipping at the Styrofoam cup. The coffee burned my tongue, and I felt wondrously wounded, alive in a new way, a way that I hadn't recognized yet. I knew enough by then to know her new man lived at 19th and Chestnut, and when I realized I stood sipping my coffee at 17th and Chestnut, I felt chilled despite the heat. What was I doing? Stalking? The word felt funny in my head, but true, and I asked myself if this was what crazy felt like—if it were something you stumbled upon on the street, something you fell into as easily as bed or love. Two blocks down, miraculously, I found the car, that fucking Accord, with a crumbled pack of Marlboros on the dash, the cigarettes confirming everything I needed to know. Her new man must have smoked. Marlboros, of all things. The Marlboro Man. Where's irony when you need it?

That's the way things worked that summer, even the disasters clicking together like a complicated puzzle. Rita didn't smoke, of course, didn't drink, didn't even know how to blow a guy when I first met her, and here she was down in Center City *doing him*, fucking this other guy, and there I stood outside of her car with his smokes on her dash, the same dash where I used to casually toss my sunglasses and pontificate about life the way only a twenty-five-year-old can pontificate about life. I thought of her blowing him then, shocked at how quickly and deeply I'd fallen, how low I could go. Something else clicked into place then, some assurance about our essential isolation, our loneliness. People don't care, not really, unless they are your people, and even then, well, here was evidence of those limits, those smokes on the dash mocking me. Remembering my father's box of stolen sausages, I giggled a bit and thought about smashing the window the way that thief had done that night. But that was a different car, a different life. Even so, if I were a different type of man, I would have done something like that, and maybe all this could have been avoided—all this messy remembering, these stories.

Stop.

WHAT I REALLY WANT to know before I die is how our lives fit together, any of ours, as one thing. What rules us, if anything, besides dumb luck, impulse, fear? Maybe it's as simple as the question itself, this need for order, for fitting our stories together into some kind of manageable whole. Otherwise, what is there? Just some guy standing on the sidewalk staring into the scorched place that once held his heart. And that was me. That Sunday standing in the street outside of Rita's car, I realized something inexplicable and strange was happening to me. I wish I could tell you about it, but I'm no Nabokov. If you want Nabokov go read Nabokov. I'm this guy, average, maybe a bit above, with a good, but reckless heart sometimes driven mad by his own dumb desires. There. That's it. I've said it all. I'm one you might never hear from again.

Let's just conclude this minor ode by saying that at the moment I saw the cigarettes on the dash, I switched, something inside of me slipped away and fizzled out forever. It was a power outage of sorts—a few seconds without electricity in the middle of the night and when you awake the next morning the red digits on the alarm clock blink twelve furiously. Midnight, or is it noon? You open your eyes and clear the sleep from your head, realizing you've missed an important appointment. That part of your life is over. Done. Now, stretch that blinking twelve, twelve, twelve o'clock over your face like a mask. The digits, your eyes. Wear it for a few years until it becomes indistinguishable from your own meaty flesh. Your smile, the Joker's. That's me, that's what happened to me. Maybe it happens to everyone, eventually. I was on and then I was off, and then it didn't matter anymore because I started moving around again, realizing I'd lost a big chunk of that other guy, the previous me—a chunk like a gap in your gums, a lost tooth, a spot in your life where you push your tongue like an eye, just to see, to feel, what isn't there anymore.

WEST PHILLY

PART OF ME STILL couldn't fathom that our life together was done, still believed we lived in that cramped third-floor apartment, two floors above the James Spader look-alike who held open mic poetry readings every Friday evening in his living room and once asked if you'd ever read *Madame Bovary*. Across the street sat the Ethiopian place, where they served our favorite—spicy lamb and vegetables. We'd eat with our hands, scooping up the meat with flat bread, a sweaty glass of pilsner by my side. You drank only water. We lived well in those rooms lined up like shot glasses— living room, kitchen, bedroom, and I wanted nothing more than that life, again and again, the way Nietzsche, the stoics, and your mother's kindness had promised.

This was the beginning of the second summer without Rita, and I suspected nothing could be as ridiculous as the first. In the fourteen months since the end, I'd already moved to Japan and back, moved in with a different girl, and then moved out. Just two months ago, a Korean deli clerk had shot a black kid, a teenager, over five dollars of quarters in the till, nearly sparking a Do-The-Right-Thing riot in this city of my birth. Now, standing in front of that same deli, the newspaper screamed more death: *Jerome Brown Gone*. Jerome, our Jerome, the defensive tackle for the Philadelphia Eagles, the team we watched together. Vivacious and lively. "Like a big kid," one of his team-mates said. "He would have made a great old man," said his coach. I'd obsessed over these same Eagles, videotaping the important games to watch again and again, even the losses, especially the losses. You had indulged me.

Instead of this, the whole sad mess, I decided to pretend. I was walking back to you waiting in our bed. Let's say the Berlin Wall had just come down and you were wearing the same I-Goldberg T-shirt you always slept in and I had slipped out early while you still snoozed. I had not read Thoreau's warning about desperate men living quietly. I had not bought into the Bloomsbury Group. I had not slept with a girl simply because I liked her haircut. I had not apologized for such, thinking, somehow, this would make my transgression OK. I had not come home one night to find you simply gone, no note, nothing. I had not pissed away a chance to live in Tokyo. I had not taken a room in a house near the University of Pennsylvania with four strangers who left weird, backbiting notes for one another taped to the fridge in the kitchen (*Please don't leave my steak knifes in the sink! Show respect and wipe the counter. Don't shave in the shower! Leave your share of the rent on table by 8 a.m.—that's when I go to the bank. Recycling every Thursday. It's your responsibility. Put items on the curb, not the porch!*). No, this was not my life. There was another story, a better one, the one in my head.

"Dollar ninety-eight," the clerk said as I placed my coffee and bagel on the counter.

I smiled, and told him I needed more—another banana nut muffin for my girlfriend waiting at home, and I paid him in dimes, nickels and pennies, the last of my money, everything that I had.

"What do you think about the wall coming down?" I asked.

He looked at me surprised that I'd extended our little exchange, a faux pas in a city where hundreds of its citizens had been murdered in the last eleven months, including the black teenager who had bled to death on the sidewalk outside this very shop, after being shot, perhaps, by this very clerk.

"Have a good day," he said.

SUNDAY MORNING IN WEST Philly, June 25. The humidity already there, but not the bad heat, not yet, it's only 80 degrees, maybe, so there's a sense of relief, refuge, and I'm feeling lighter inside this coolness, inside this game in my head as the starlings sing, their beaks yellow for the summer, the purple energy of a Saturday night lingering in the air, the disease of it too, splattered there on the sidewalk and in puddles along the curb, the blood and the vomit and the cum, Philly's sick soup. I felt like some kind of bobble-headed mystic, a dime-store cross between Tiny Tim and Jim Morrison. My people had sprung from this stretch of blocks, my dad's people, his parents—a Catholic and a Jew. When they married, each of their families had shunned the other, and I was left leaning on the Catholic side. I knew none of this that day, of course, such knowledge wouldn't come for years, in the week before I left for Montana as if I'd finally earned the story, when my cousin, who managed a liquor store and liked pot as much as she liked wine, asked, "Didn't you know grandfather was Jewish?"

When I shook my head no, stoned from her weed, she laughed and said, "It's true. He married for love and had to say goodbye to his family. I don't know if I could do that. Would you?"

Up ahead, like Ahab, I spied a yellow Volkswagen Beetle—Rita's model and color—parked in the street. I believed then, as I do now, that you are given some things only once in this life—to ask for it again is greedy and useless, but as I sauntered up next to the car that morning and peered down through the side window to see a shoebox full of tapes on the passenger's seat, breathless with excitement, I smiled, kept moving, the sight of the tapes some secret red thrill, an affirmation of sorts, a promise that it might just be OK, that batshit crazy or drunk every night by nine were not my only options, that some other avenue might present itself.

It was only when I didn't make the light on Chestnut Street that I stopped, turned around and sensed the darkness trailing—the stupid, selfish shit we do. We are. It washed over me with the clarity of a truth: This was fucked up. A pair of Converse sneakers hung by their laces from the telephone wires above my head, relics, like the car, from an earlier age. Rita had sold her Bug a couple of years ago, replacing it with a sky-blue Accord, so as I stood there watching a few early morning cars cruise pass I decided the only thing I could do was circle back and doubledown, try again. Do this pretending business better.

Now there was a song in my head—The Cure's "Pictures of You." A pie wedge of morning sky peeked through the roofs of the houses and trees, and the sun on the back of my neck felt like something between a slap and a kiss. I walked along, passing pigeons croaking and strutting, proud and crazy, a frayed poster for a band, Go to Blazes, stapled to a telephone pole: "Friday Night at the Khyber," and an ancient woman in a babushka pulling along a white poodle she called Charles. "Charles, this way, Charles. Charles, don't touch that. Oh, Charles." I came up on the Volkswagen again, and this time pulled the car door opened, and in a gesture full of foolishness and hope, I reached in, grabbed the shoebox of tapes, shut the door, and stepped away. Kept moving.

Box in hand, expecting someone to yell after me, for

Charles to nip and yap at the heel of my Doc Martens, for some cop to pull up next to me, "Hey, buddy, what do you got there," I just kept walking. No one noticed me, of course, and two blocks later I barely glanced up at the house where we had shared that life, passing, too, The Red Sea restaurant, where we had eaten among the Ethiopians, our whiteness exotic to them, the men at the bar taking quick glances at your blonde hair, the three empty beer glasses in front of me, another one coming.

I felt giddy and dead, hustling my way home to the house where I had the room overlooking an alley, an ancient junkyard door propped on cinder blocks as a desk, piles of paperbacks and clothes. A white cat. When I made the top of the stairs, Gloria, steak-knife owner and recycler extraordinaire, popped out of the bathroom we shared, glanced down at the box I was holding and then back up into my eyes. Caught. Thief and liar. Fool and loser. Gloria wore an orange velour robe, her hair up in a towel. Without her glasses, and the line of her mouth free from her worry over cutlery and the environment, she was almost pretty. Could she be my destiny?

"Hey."

"Hey."

What I wanted to tell her, but didn't, was yet another story, an even better one, the one about the thief who broke into Rita's Beetle on Christmas Eve, our first Christmas together, and how I found it kind of funny, this grinch-crook getting what he deserved: one imitation leather wallet holding two dollars, my license, an expired video rental care for Joe's Video, the ticket stubs from our first date together (*My Beautiful Laundrette*), as well as those lame gifts I'd purchased for my family in a one-stop shopping spree at the Gallery Mall—a polyester ski hat, fruity scarf, paisley tie, and a Hickory Farm box of assorted cheeses for the old man. This, to me, was hilarious. Cosmic justice. But Rita? Rita was furious, righteously so, and demanded blood, Old Testament justice, so despite the Christmas day, we'd called the cops and reported the theft and waited almost an hour in our cold vestibule, sipping bad coffee, waiting for the officers to pull up in their patrol car, all of which saved me about a year later when I received a notice in the mail to appear in traffic court for not paying a moving violation for the Yellow Cab I was driving one night on Vine Street.

Here's the twist: I showed up in traffic court with my father, but the presiding judge had no interest in my excuses, immediately dressing me down as immature, self-ish, a child. The judge had glanced at my father, his white hair and false teeth, the six foot of him in blue work shirt and tie, and said he deserved better than me for a son. Done with her lecture, she finally asked, "What do you have to say for yourself, Mr. Simmons."

In one sense she was spot on, this Judge Judy, and I could have nodded and taken the punishment, maybe should have, but instead I told her the truth—I explained how my bag had been stolen from my girlfriend's car a couple years back and the bag held my wallet, and in the wallet, my license, and the man driving the Yellow Cab was not me, but just some other guy posing as me. With my license.

The judge stared at me for a hard five seconds, waiting for a smile or a chuckle, some crack in the veneer of my story, but I lowered my head and kept my smirk to myself.

"Police report?" she asked.

Rita's Christmas anger flashed in my mind as I handed the sheet to the bailiff who walked over to the judge, the keys on his belt jiggling, his gut hanging over his belt like another piece of evidence. The judge read the report in silence, dismissed the case without looking up.

"Next," she said.

Afterwards, my father and I were joyous, full of pride at how we had beaten the system by following its own rules, purchasing celebratory meatball sandwiches sprinkled with parmesan cheese from a sidewalk cart and washing them down with cold cans of Cokes on a cement bench outside the 30th Street Post Office, where Dad worked as the Superintendent of Registered Mail. He had to eat and hustle inside to a room caged off from the rest of the post office because of the expensive mail it held, and I had to walk across 30th Street to the train station and take the train back to Bala Cynwyd where Rita waited. Yes, we had left the city by then.

"That was good," Dad said. "Really good. Thank Rita for that police report."

On the train, I thought of the man who'd ended up with my license. Most likely he wasn't the man who had stolen the bag and the wallet, but an immigrant without a green card trying to start a life here by driving a cab, someone who had purchased the license on the black market. Maybe from India, maybe we looked somewhat alike—in the vicinity of height and weight and age. I considered his eyes, their color.

In West Philly that day, Gloria, my roommate, went back to her room—the tail end of her orange robe dragging across the wooden floor as if she were Queen Elizabeth, and in my room, I called my father. I asked if he'd heard the news about Jerome Brown, the dead football player, the Eagle. He had.

"Why drive like that with a boy in the car?" he said, not

really asking me anything.

My father said it was no tragedy for Jerome Brown, but for his young nephew who was in the car at the time of the crash and who had also died. The nephew was eleven. Dad, like the judge, was right but wrong too. It was an accident, and years later when he fell down the basement steps of my sister's house and hit his head on the cement floor to die, I didn't think of Jerome Brown, but one final story about my mother's father, not the Jew, but the drunk, an Irish one, a man in his grave before I was born.

This other grandfather's wife had to take the trolley each Friday to the factory where he worked to pick up his paycheck. Apparently, Dad told me, there were dozens of wives who showed up like this, each Friday to get their husband's checks, to make sure they didn't drink them up in one night. My grandfather worked at the Ford factory in North Philly, toiling on the assembly line, hinging doors to a car's chassis, again and again, eight hours at a time, a job that required little skill, but endurance, strength, repetitive lifting of metal, fifty or sixty pounds of it, and he made decent money doing it, actually kept his wife and seven children clothed, fed, and under one roof. My grandfather was a large man at least six-foot-five, maybe 250 pounds, hands like catcher's mitts. Once, Dad told me, he fell in the tub, drunk, and my father and three others were summoned to help lift the old man up and out, and my father described my grandfather's naked legs in great detail as if this were the point of the story, which maybe it was. Bloated like soggy wood, broken tree limbs dug from the dirt, an explosion of blue and red veins protruding from his thighs like lines on a globe, thighs like small countries. Slick with water and who knew what else.

"He was a mess, old Andy," Dad said. "But as much as

he drank, and he drank every day starting in the morning when he sent his four daughters off to the church down the block so he could get into his cups in peace, he never missed work."

I've missed work. Plenty of it.

And now, years later, it occurs to me I don't know where this grandfather is buried, this man a drunk too, nor have I visited my own father's grave since the day of his funeral when I placed my hand flat against the bronze of his casket as they lowered his ridiculous cigar-shaped canister into the ground and I stood there watching my palm sweat linger on the metal in the hot August sun. I wanted it to mean something, that sweat, and I could say that I like to think my father felt the touch, that I imagine the handprint still there underneath all that dirt, but those are just lies, things to say in a story. The truth is I live too far away to visit the grave. It would take a special trip to see my dad now, to glimpse Philadelphia again, my home place, and some part of me doesn't think any of it is worth it. But another part of me, maybe the part writing this, knows that some day I'll make it home. I have to. One way or the other I'll get home to swim once more in all these stories.

WHY DON'T YOU KILL ME?

MY WOMAN LEFT ME and I thought my life was over even though I was just a babe at twenty-five. This was in Philly, years ago, and with Rita gone, I'd taken work as a waiter at the Frog, an upscale catering joint that served the city's best parties. It was not dull work, but it dulled the mind, and doing it burned off energy in a way that I liked and thought maybe I needed. What I remember most clearly about that time is how the stink of failure clung to me, like gum to a shoe, and made my ill-fitting second-hand polyester tuxedo feel just right, made standing behind the Franklin Institute science museum with a team of elegantly disheveled waiters dumping greasy garbage bags full of potato skins, spare ribs, cheese sauces, coffee grounds, and soiled napkins feel so right. The museum's own deep-fried cafeteria runoff had stewed all day in the industrial-sized dumpsters, so by the time we arrived near midnight the smell of it—rank, eggy, almost sweet—ran right up inside, tickling the linings of my nose and bringing bile to the back of my throat. I didn't mind, though, because it was simple: I'd loved Rita and she was gone, and as I tossed down those slimy bags into the dumpsters, each bag landing with a satisfying thud, it sounded exactly like pieces of a new me clicking into place.

We smoked as we worked. Bathed in the drone of three massive generators that fueled the museum, Liz, Runner, Churchill and I bitched and moaned and joked, smoking under a milky, moonless city sky.

"Watch this," Runner said, hoisting a bag onto his

shoulder, before he spun three times and tossed it into the deepest part of the dumpster where it crunched atop some glass.

"Bulls-eye," he shouted. "Those fools always put the glass in the back."

The museum covered a full city block. Steps of polished granite led to an entrance lined with Greco-Roman columns. Inside, over 1,500 exhibits filled its cavernous rooms. Sir Isaac's Loft, Mummies of Egypt, How Electricity Changed the World, Next Stop Mars. During the day, tourists wandered in by the busloads, but at night when the museum was rented for catered affairs and two or three parties could be going on at once on different floors, the Frog's staff had the run of the place, and doing such grueling work among the eclectic blend of exhibits weirdly transformed the place into part wonderland, part torture chamber.

The work reminded me of my teenage gig at the Colonial Inn where my good friend Paul Cavanaugh, who turned me on to pot, would sneak off to the dumpsters and suck out the compressed air of six empty whip cream canisters in rapid succession. Whippets, he explained. The act bathed his brain in nitrous oxide, leaving his mind beautifully washed out and pink, moments Paul, one of the smartest guys I'd ever met, described as "euphoric, very pure, like dancing inside a bubble." Along with weed, he introduced me to Oxford shirts and the coolness of nerdy intellectualism—though I never had the balls to try a whippet. (Paul was also, I think, a little in love with me, and I was drawn to him, especially his willingness to exchange brain cells for a few seconds of cheap fun.) After sucking out the cans, he'd stand wobbling on the ledge, his bony features a collage of joy, fear, and some kind of ravenous hunger that even then, I knew, could never be satisfied.

That night by the dumpsters, despite the February frost, we lingered. The chore of cleaning up after 250 accountants waited inside. John Churchill, who claimed a distant lineage to the British prime minister, a lie none of us believed, held court.

"Fifty-two percent of Americans have an alias of some kind," he explained. "Not just a nickname, but a name they assume when the situation suits them."

"A pseudonym," Liz said. "That's what I need."

We were a mixed brew of budding artists, actors, and writers—gay and straight, black and white—all of us pretenders in one way or the other, all of us trying to be anything but the waiters we were. Churchill was a bit of an exception. A buttoned-down white guy, straight, a business major, but in his own way he was as eccentric as anyone else who worked the Frog.

"I can totally see what you're saying," Runner said. "Half my uncles, I don't even know their real names."

"What's your real name?" I asked.

"I'd like to disappear for a week," Liz said, lazily tipping her head back to blow out a stream of smoke trailed by the puffs of her own condensed breath. "Or maybe just drop out one week a month. I couldn't imagine just going away forever, you know. I like too many people to totally just disappear."

"Yeah, there's that," I said, vaguely, "but there's always people around, right? Wherever you go there's got to be some new folks."

"Folks? What are you—one of The Beverley Hillbillies," Runner said.

"Whatever. People. Humans. Warm bodies," I said.

"My dog's a warm body, but he doesn't need anyone," Liz said.

"He needs you," I said. "Dogs need people."

"Not mine, remember. He's part wolf."

Liz and I had slept together a few times but weren't doing that anymore. It wasn't a big deal. Everyone screwed everyone else at the Frog—possibly, almost certainly, because everyone *was* someone else at the Frog. Runner was an actor, funny and rude, and I think he'd hooked up with Liz a few times too. Liz herself was a student-painter at the Pennsylvania Academy of the Fine Arts, an achingly beautiful girl with the translucent skin of a child or a saint. Her wolf-dog, she had told me, was spooked by strangers and sudden movements. She feared that one day he would bolt from her and terrorize the city, though she once explained wolves were the gentlest of creatures—just loners. "Like you," she'd said to me, kissing my cheek and telling me goodbye before telling me she was the type of person who liked "to do things," whatever that meant. It had been that night when we stopped sleeping together.

"Who's talking about disappearing?" Runner said.

"One out of five girls under the ages of ten are victims of abduction or attempted abductions," Churchill said.

"Who are you, man, with these statistics?" Runner asked. "And what are you trying to tell us?"

"The truth," Churchill said. "Just the truth."

The truth? My truth, as mordant and ordinary as the next guy's, involved Rita, my first love, how our life together had somehow slid down a rabbit hole known only to the young and tender-hearted, how it had simultaneously disappeared and grown more substantial in the nearly two years since we'd split—a fact I couldn't process, couldn't understand, and which, frankly, was driving me a little nuts. What had happened to the party where we'd first met? That Thanksgiving dinner at her mother's when the Eagles had shut out the Cowboys and I'd drunk my first glass of tomato juice? The place on Chestnut Street where we'd go for drinks and a talk? That time we ran home from the bar and made love in the kitchen while the mac-n-cheese burned on the stove? Those days felt at once as weightless and impossible as dreams and as real as the coins in my pocket. During our courtship, we'd zigzagged across the city in Rita's yellow VW Bug, talking about music, books, our families. I'd told her about my mom. One secret Rita shared was her virginity. Nearly twenty and a virgin, I'd never rushed her, not once, and when that moment finally did arrive, nearly a year into our relationship, Rita had squeezed her eyes shut and grimaced as we moved ourselves together. This in my boyhood bed that I'd lugged to my first apartment, a West Philly efficiency with a bug problem.

"Does it hurt?" I'd whispered, touching her hair, kissing her eye lids, ready to weep with how much I loved this girl.

"Keep going," she'd said, tears at the corners of her eyes. "Just keep going."

EARLIER THAT NIGHT AT the museum, I'd helped out behind the bar, mostly running for ice, until a pinch-faced drunk had ordered two gin and tonics. "Pronto," he'd said, snapping his fingers.

When I'd handed him the drinks, he smirked and said, "Hey, thanks, guy, those are some pretty finely-poured drinks. How do you get a job like this? You got to know someone or what?"

I'd turned away without a word, happy that I wasn't locked down into a life where happy meant getting drunk at office parties and insulting the help. The truth was we took a strange pride in our work at the Frog, thinking, deep down, that we were better than the people we served simply because we'd stayed free of the buttoned-down, nine-to-five grind that kept them caged like monkeys.

The party that night was in the main rotunda where marble floors gleamed beneath a twenty-ton stone sculpture of Ben Franklin. Franklin, decked in his colonial garb, had a stern, brooding look on his face, a look intended to portend great thoughts, though we all thought Ben looked as if he were in the middle of a giant, blissful shit.

"He's the Buddha of this place," Churchill always joked. "The Buddha of America."

Mainly, though, what we did at the Frog was work, and working usually meant orchestrating a party for hundreds from scratch, showing up in street clothes hours before the gig began to set up tables and chairs, food stations and bars, before changing into our tuxedos and serving hors d'oeuvres, salad, the main entrée, dessert and coffee, and then, drunk from exhaustion, or sometimes just drunk from the cocktails we'd imbibed on the sly, we broke it all down and packed it away as if none of it had happened in the first place. We felt like magicians, performing acts of transformation bookended by stacks of chairs and banquet tables—stacking, rolling, and unfolding only to fold, roll and stack a few hours later. The self-proclaimed dykes loved this part of the job, and they would strip down to their undershirts and sports bras to show off their tribal tattoos, their tight biceps, while most of the gay boys sashayed around trying to avoid any heavy lifting—us straight guys caught somewhere in the middle, our masculinity a joke, a middle-class cliché we did our best to hide.

The best job, though, was bartending. It required the least amount of hustle and heavy lifting, while offering the most autonomy—to say nothing of the free booze. I wanted to be a bartender. It was a goal I had in those days. We all stole the top-shelf liquor and premium wine that the Frog served, and the stolen hooch always turned up magically at our after-hour parties, and it was those parties that gave our work its real meaning—kept us coming back for more. They were fantastic, these affairs, almost wistful, drinking top-shelf vodka and hundred-dollar bottles of wine among people who pretended for a living—perfect company for a guy like me, a mixed Jew-bird from the burbs dragging along his own chained heart as he tried to figure out his next move.

AFTER DINNER THAT NIGHT, but before we went to the dumpsters, in the long drowsy lull between dinner and dessert when the guests were mostly drunk and somewhat content, I'd drifted away from the rotunda and wandered up to the atrium, where the best exhibits were housed. A pendulum hung from a cable stretched down the center of a spiral staircase that led to the atrium. From the fourth floor to the first, three hundred feet in all, the ball hung, rocking slowly back-and-forth. At the bottom of the stairs, not far from the pendulum, was a gigantic fiberglass replica of the human heart. This heart had a set of metal steps that twisted from the left ventricle up through the hollowed chamber into the aorta before spiraling down through the right ventricle. The two-beat, da-dump, da-dump, da-dump, of an actual beating heart amplified the chamber as did a recorded voice intoning all the necessary biological facts—*the human heart beats on average two billion times per lifetime...*

I'd sat for a few minutes inside the pulse and throb of the fiberglass heart, considering Rita and her ways, how she'd marched in one April morning to announce, "I'm moving out," and that, as they say, was that. She hadn't come home at all the previous evening, and I'd waited up most of the night and early morning, my mind sweating out roadside atrocities, brutal abductions, vicious assaults—all the things she'd feared about living in the city—until, finally, I fell into a fitful sleep, dreaming, insipidly, of her coming home holding two steaming mugs of hot chocolate. When she plowed into our apartment, I was so happy just to see her breathing that I'd heard hardly a word of what she'd said, and gave little thought to where she'd slept or with whom.

"Did you hear me?" she'd said, brushing off my touch. "I'm moving out."

"But you're home, you're home. You're OK."

"Did you hear me?"

A WEEK BEFORE THE party at the institute, at a gala in Gladwyne for board members of the Philadelphia Art Museum, a wealthy woman's purse had been stolen and our maitre d', Don, a large, square-shouldered, handsome man with sad, droopy James-Baldwin eyes—a man whose dick I'd supposedly sucked, a man who once had been married with kids before leaving his marriage for a gay lover, a lover who had gone on to die of AIDS—lined us up in the kitchen and demanded that the thief step forward.

When none of the staff fessed up, we went reluctantly back to our business. It was another bitterly cold night in a series of bitterly cold nights, and I was out back in an alley, alone, dumping ice from the bartenders' bins into the gutter, kicking at the clumps to loosen them, my fingers and knuckles burning with the cold when the black purse appeared among the ice like a glowing chunk of coal. My breath quickened, and at once I realized I was about to lose my job, which wasn't a bad thought, but the idea of losing it for a crime I didn't commit filled me with a type of dread and outrage I didn't entirely understand. I started yelping like an ape, and for one brief, wobbly moment, I thought I'd actually stolen the purse and somehow forgotten it, as if some phantom me had slipped inside the lining of my life, pulled down the mask, and was waiting there now, inside, as this other me, the real one, yelped for it to get out, to leave me alone.

Liz was there then. She'd heard me and had come running to help. She stood behind me, peeking over my shoulder, her breath smoky on my neck, as we stared down at the purse, which I couldn't bring myself to touch. She whispered urgently into my ear, telling me to pick it up and get rid of it, and I began to do so when Don appeared around the corner of the building wearing his shiniest of smiles. His dark tuxedo looked purple against his skin, and he looked me in the eye for the briefest of moments before plucking the purse from my hands and turning away without a word.

"What the fuck," I squealed to Liz. "Do you think he thinks I took it?"

"What? No, you're fine," Liz said, laughing. "Don loves you, everyone knows that."

She'd heard the story.

In August, during my first few months at the Frog, Don had taken a few of his best boys, myself included, back to his house in Germantown that he shared with his mother. She was asleep when we arrived after two, closer to 3:00 a.m. We'd settled into the den at the back of the house drinking our stolen Stoli and telling our stories. At one point, as I came back from the bathroom, Don cornered me in the hallway where there were a few framed photographs on the walls, photographs of his grandparents, his mother's people. Sharecroppers from Virginia, Don said, telling me his great-grandfather was the son of a free Northerner, but that his mother's side were slaves. He pointed to a photo of the family matriarch, his mother's grandmother, gently tracing the outline of this woman's face on the glass frame covering it. I didn't understand what he wanted from me, what I could possibly offer, so I just looked at the photograph. The woman's face was proud and fierce with dark eyes and a huge forehead, a face that said simply: *I have suffered and I have survived. I am this.* Now I must tell you, Don was not what he seemed. He was not liked by the majority of the servers because of his sarcasm and his toughness, but mostly because he was suspected of skimming hundreds from tips meant for us, but the way he touched that glass frame showed a type of tender grace that surprised me. It felt like a secret, an offering, as we spoke there in the hallway, his face so close to mine that I could see the beginnings of his beard, smell his licorice breath.

We'd just worked a pool party in Villanova—twelve long hours in the sun, punctuated by a rain shower—and part of what passed between Don and me was surely nothing more than shared exhaustion, but there was something else too, something deeper, something inside the silence we let hang between us. It was as if we had glimpsed each other hiding within ourselves. Either one of us could have opened the door of the other and sauntered in, but a burst of laughter rang out from the den, and we drifted back toward the others.

At the pool party earlier that afternoon (a Sweet Sixteen for a CEO's daughter), as the Frog's four-star chef grilled sirloin, shrimp and vegetables in the makeshift kitchen we'd set up in the client's garage, Don had talked juicily about coming nine times the night before, and I wondered how and why he had counted and what exactly he thought about when he thought about his dead lover. Midway through the party, the rain had begun and we used garbage bags to protect ourselves, making ponchos of the bags by poking a head-hole and two arm-holes in the green plastic, and slipping it over our tuxedos. We looked like idiots but felt like gods, misplaced and cursed to wander this earth for a few short years before we assumed our rightful place.

Earlier that day, before the rain, it'd been so hot that the client had let us take off our jackets—a rare favor granted. The party was mostly rich, nice-looking white girls in biki-nis, girls who didn't even see us—even when we wore the trash-bag ponchos, which we all thought were hilarious. And here's the point: I loved the way the parties made me invis-ible, how Rita would finally slip from my mind as easily as the dream she'd become. It felt like those first few moments of wakefulness, free from the stranglehold of memory, sim-ilar, I imagine, to the bliss Paul Cavanaugh felt swaying by those dumpsters at the Colonial Inn. I knew if I could string enough of those moments together I would be OK. I might find my way out.

At first, Rita wouldn't admit she'd been with another guy, but I knew the score. Somehow, I'd forgotten how to fuck her, to love her that way. His name was Vijay, this guy she worked with at Temple, where she'd started taking French classes even though she already had an Engineering degree and a job, a good one. She'd dropped his name a few times in the previous weeks, and all I could imagine doing was joke about it. "Vijay? What kind of name is Vijay?" It was Indian, I learned, and after she'd left, I'd envisioned them twisted together in positions from the *Kama Sutra*, knees above shoulders, tongue there, a belly kissing the ceiling, all sorts of delicious things.

What else can I say?

The first time I saw Rita she was in the sun wearing white as I sat nearby in the grass listening to a cassette tape, *Kiss Me Kiss Me Kiss Me*. She'd just parked her yellow Beetle, and when I saw her my heart sort of shouted. She smiled, shouting back, "You like The Cure?" and we were together, more or less, for the next five years. Later that evening, wooing her at a corner table beneath a framed print of a clown, I'd plucked an orange from a fruit bowl and compared it to her, saying something about peeling it, my reference obvious, lame, really, but somehow winning her still. She wanted me, I guess. Maybe she noticed the way my voice cracked as I told my story or how my fingers trembled as I made my lame joke. I don't know, and never will, but she saw me, somehow, and I her. It's no more complicated than that. We let the other in—as simple and impossible as that can be.

AT THE DUMPSTERS THAT night, after Churchill and Runner had gone back inside, Liz and I lingered.

"People know what happened between you and Don," she said. "Is that why he let you off about the purse?"

"I don't know," I said, not really understanding what had happened, which didn't happen with Don, but another guy, a fellow waiter named Darrell who supplied me with drinks and sucked my dick before I stopped him and got down on my knees and placed his dick into my mouth. It wasn't so much about desire—at least not in the way I'd experienced it with women, as some type of sharing, it was just about getting off, about feeling the naked monkey touch of another. It's what I liked most about men, how easily they admitted their desires, how simple they made it—two bodies, this one next to yours, warm and excited, a few moments of electricity.

"It doesn't matter," Liz said.

"It's not even what happened," I said.

But I liked Liz, I did, and she didn't believe me, and that's what hurt more than people talking about Don and me.

"What did happen then?"

"Nothing, really," I said looking at her in the eyes. "It was with Darrell. Just a couple of times."

She got mad then, which I didn't understand, because for once I was being honest. Was it because she'd heard about Don but not Darrell? Was Don OK, but Darrell somehow wrong? I can only guess. All I know is how important she was to me at that moment, standing there in the cold by the dumpsters under the washed out light of a city sky. She was everything to me, and though I only spoke to her a few times after this night, I'm still there, over twenty years later, part of me still waits by those dumpsters, gray moon watching, hoping for a moment of recognition.

"You know, you don't really belong here," Liz said, finally.

"Why?"

"Because you're just fooling around, fucking with people."

"How am I fucking with people?"

She didn't answer.

"You're the one I liked," I said.

"No I'm not," she said. "But it doesn't matter. We'd better get back inside and start cleaning up."

NEAR THE END OF our relationship, after I had deceived her, Rita had gotten so mad at me once that halfway home, after picking my drunken ass up from a bar in downtown Philly, she'd yanked her car to the side of the street and told me to get out. See, we'd made this deal when we agreed to move out of the city—she'd pick me up downtown after the trains had stopped running, but that day she'd had enough.

"Get out of the fucking car," she screamed, her features contorted. A face I didn't recognize, a mask. We were somewhere in the bowels of West Philly. I told her I didn't know where I was, but she didn't believe me or didn't care.

"Get out," she screamed again. "Just get out of the car."

I got out and began walking this long road, but three blocks later found myself in a pickle when a kid jogged up behind me and shoved a stick in a paper bag under my chin and told me to give him my wallet. I told him I didn't have a wallet and he said he wasn't fooling, that he'd just seen me take my wallet from my hip pocket and put it in the inside breast pocket of the vintage herringbone blazer I favored in those days. He was right. I had just done that, thinking stupidly, that the person following me might try to *pickpocket* me.

So I gave the guy my wallet. Maybe it was a gun in the bag. Maybe it wasn't. I asked if he'd do me a favor, if he'd take the money and give me back the wallet, my license.

"You know how much of a fucking hassle it is to get a new license," I said.

He looked at me, looked in the wallet. He took out a dollar, the lone bill in the fold, and a joint, or what I thought was a joint, something I'd purchased from another guy earlier that night at a bar. He looked at me again, shaking his head now. I asked if he wanted to smoke it.

"Smoke this?" he said.

He unrolled the fake joint—it was just rolling paper rolled within rolling paper—and laughed at me. I was sitting on the curb at this point, and he still held the paper bag, but he wasn't pointing it at me any longer. All pretense was gone. I was a fool; he was a thief with a fake gun—this was the truth, and something of its kind hovered between Don and me the night he showed me the picture of his great-grandmother. The same thing hung between Liz and me by the dumpsters, and maybe even between me and the person I was becoming the night I found that purse in the ice.

I worked at the Frog for almost two years and it forced me to remake the city, refashion it into a place where I might again begin to live. We held our parties in private homes as well as public spaces: parks, zoos, museums, aquariums, and what I did in those places sort of saved me because I began to see different lives, different possibilities spiraling out from my own silly, selfish choices. And as I helped transform those places, I began to wonder if I could transform myself, if there were a better way to be me, better versions waiting for this old one, this old me, to catch up. Maybe it's what I heard that night with my friends as the trash bags dropped into the dumpster, what might have begun the night Rita kicked me from her Accord or even that day I waited for her at the Love statue, sick with love and lust. Or maybe it was always there, waiting.

"Where am I?" I'd called after the thief as he walked away.

Honestly, I can't remember what he said, if anything. Perhaps he just kept walking, thinking God knows what, but what I like to think happened was he turned back to me and shouted, "You're not in Kansas, anymore."

And he was right.

FISHTOWN

A FEW DAYS BEFORE my father came to help me vacate my Fishtown loft, I hurried past the mouth of an alley where I spotted a woman in a glittery blue skirt kneeling before a man, her face collapsed into his lap. The man wore a puffy orange jacket and held his hand flat atop the woman's skull, directing her mouth up and down the length of his dick. This was 1993, and I'd only recently moved to Fishtown from a house in South Philly that I'd shared with a Jewish girl from Cherry Hill. Things between us were OK, we were just roommates, until she asked me to move out when I began bringing home a dark-skinned girl from Center City on a regular basis. What could I do? I moved out. The girl owned the house, or her mother did, and my new friend wasn't exactly welcomed in South Philly, so I took my act to Fishtown, to a loft there in a converted warehouse filled with wannabe artists, creative types and the like—people like me.

When my father had first seen the loft, he looked around, stunned, shaking his head and chuckling. I can still hear that chuckle today. There was sawdust on the floor and a toilet/shower combo stood in the middle of the room with no walls for privacy. In fact, there were no real walls anywhere—only two plywood sheets sectioning off a corner of the space for a bedroom. The space was completely open, and just creepy enough that I began receiving prank phone calls from a guy who said he could spy me through the industrial-sized windows of my loft, windows covered by only a wire mesh, no curtains. This joker said he liked to jerk off as he watched me pad around barefoot, and once even described what I was wearing as I listened to him breath heavily into the phone. When he did that, I hung up the phone, switched off the lights, checked the deadbolt on the front door and crawled into bed, where I still didn't feel safe, not really, because there was no lock on the sliding industrial door between my place and the adjacent loft. I'd jerry-rigged the thing shut with some bungee cords and rope, but if you wanted it opened you could get it open, and, occasionally, I did just that, sliding it open to wander around my neighbor's loft when she was out, picking up her comb and toothbrush, smelling her clothes, and examining her work—these minuscule landscape paintings, oils on canvases about the size of a top of a shoebox, swirling colors reminiscent of Van Gogh, quite beautiful, and when I gazed down into them I got this feeling inside that everything would be OK.

Now, five months after Dad's first visit, he was back, helping me move out. I moved a lot in those days, but Dad was a bit early that morning and was calling from a pay phone down the block. He needed me to come down and open the front gate of the courtyard of the warehouse. The problem was the boy I'd invited back to my place last night hadn't yet left. In fact, he was in my bed, his back to me, sticky with sleep, and he was snoring slightly through his mouth as I whispered to Dad over phone, "Give me a couple of minutes, OK, and I'll be right down."

I hung up the phone and shook my friend awake.

"Darrell, you have to get up now, that's my father. He's here. He's coming right over."

"Oh, good, I love meeting the parents," Darrell said, grinning and sitting up to rub the sleep from his eyes.

"No, Darrell, cut the shit. You have to leave right now."

My dad showed up five minutes later with his Wawa coffee and *Daily News* tucked under his arm. Did he suspect anything back then? Could he have known that I was sleeping with both boys and girls, or that when I was a boy I'd found those books he'd kept in the bottom drawer by his bed, the one with the football coach massaging the dick of his star player, books, that at first, I took to be my mother's, until I asked myself why would she keep such things and why in the dresser on *Dad's* side of the bed? When it clicked into place, I'd considered if this were the secret that had trailed after my father all his life? Was this why he hadn't received Communion for the first fifteen years of my life? Why my parents went thirteen years into their marriage before their first child?

I'm guessing we fooled each other our entire lives, Dad and I. Essentially, we were the same, and I identified with him completely, saw the world much as he did—minus the fact that I'd decided to build my life around my writing, while my father, a practical man, told me, "Son, people like us don't write books."

Even so, back then, I'm betting that Dad, a city guy at heart, enjoyed visiting me in Philadelphia, and maybe even liked helping me move from place to place. It gave him a chance to visit the city of his birth, to breathe in the exhaust and the sweat, to stand loose on a street corner and watch the people go by just as he did when he was a younger man—until he had lucked into his desk job at the postal service and moved his family to the suburbs. He was 49-years-old when he'd left Philly for good. The same age I am now.

On the morning Dad came to Fishtown to help me move, I'd rushed Darrell down to the courtyard and out the front gate, yanking the gate closed too quickly, so quickly that it clanged off my skull and jolted my hungover brain hard enough that I'd felt I'd just might faint. Darrell had stood there and laughed. I can still hear that laugh as well—almost an echo of my father's chuckle when he first saw the loft—and as I shooed Darrell down the street, he just kept laughing. He was still laughing as he passed my father coming around the corner in the opposite direction, but Dad, street-wise and all-business, offered only a crisp nod and kept walking, smiling broadly and shaking his head when he saw me waiting at the gate. "Son," he said, "I'm glad you're moving out of this neighborhood. There's too many wiseguys around here."

THE WILDWOODS

WE SAW EACH OTHER at the literacy center where you worked and I volunteered, and where later I'd meet Fiona and that whole chapter opened up, but first there was you, right then, the moment I spotted you coming down the steps at the literacy center, you smiling your red-lipstick smile, your silky dress swinging. Naomi. Your hair was still cut short, you still wore patchouli, and you were still the girl I screwed that night (and a few others) instead of coming home to Rita, my real girl, and it's one night that stands out from all the others—the night we were on your roof above your attic bedroom when you told me how all the bread trucks rumbling through that part of West Philly were really spies and I'd laughed and said, faux dramatically, that I either wanted to strip or jump, making you giggle so much that we climbed below to your room, to your futon splayed on the floor, and fucked for the first time the way only the young and naïve can fuck, as if we were the first to do something so silly, shortsighted, and selfish.

It's this night on the rooftop that I was thinking of when, four years later—a lifetime to people our age, we ended up together again in a motel room down the Jersey Shore at the tail-end of a long winter. It was Feb 25, 1993, and Rita had been gone for exactly two years, six months, and five days, each day a mini lifetime, and I'd already been to Japan and back, already lived, loved and broken up with another girl, but none of that mattered because we were somewhere Rita would never go (at least not with me). When we were together I would beg her to take us to Wildwood when we returned home late from the bars, me drunk as a bum and she as sober as a nun, but when I got that way, she'd simply laugh, shut off her car, and start up to our apartment. She never understood the romance of the ocean in winter, of doing something stupid just because you were young and could afford to do something stupid.

So there we were down the Shore, not so young anymore, me between your legs, my tongue fat on your clit, where I'd always wanted to put it during those nights in your attic bedroom but had been too timid to try. But you weren't moving as I touched you down there, and I quickly realized you weren't exactly enjoying it either, but I didn't know how to stop doing what I was doing without deflating the whole enterprise—the motel, the beach in winter, so I kept at it, obligatory, for a few more minutes, and in those sad minutes we became everything that had lured me away from Rita in the first place—the predictable, commonplace, the routine—as I had not yet learned how to handle that side of love—so I just kept kissing your pussy thinking that in another moment something might click and you would grip my cheeks with your thighs, giggling, just as Rita did when I did this to her.

But you didn't. So I stopped.

"WHAT ARE YOU DOING here?" I'd asked that day on the steps at the literacy center.

"I work here now, part-time," you said, touching the bottom strands of your dyed-black blunt cut. "But I'm thinking of something else, maybe medical school."

"Really?"

"Or would that be selling out?"

And it seemed too quickly we'd returned to this conversation about selling out or remaining true to your anarchist ideals. I'd yet to realize exactly how ashamed you were of your family's money. Over dinner that evening at an Indian place in West Philly, I told you about Rita leaving me, and you spoke of how Doug (your old flame with the withered hand who had been in Europe when we first got together) had done the same to you a year earlier, but that was all we said about their departures. But a week later, in that motel room down The Shore, when I finally stopped that business between your legs, I looked up at you, caught your eyes, and something of our old selfishness passed between us. It was quick and silent, but we finally admitted we were more alike than we cared to consider—we were people who'd hurt deeply people who'd loved us just because we could, and now here we were in a bed in an anonymous motel room in Wildwood in the middle of February, just because we could.

It made no sense and it made perfect sense, but we were still young and smart enough to realize that the past was the past and we were also lucky to be there that evening, together and warm in that bed as the snow fell outside, so I got up along your body, our bellies rubbing together like two hands, and went into you as big and gently as I could. You gasped and smiled and breathed my name into my ear in that way only you could. We rocked slowly like that for a few moments, loving each other, before a loud thump from the hallway brought us back to our more private selves and I slipped out of you, our moment gone, and you sighed and lay your head on my chest, maybe hearing my heart, maybe not, and I smelled the raspberry of your hair and sensed in a deep-dick way that I would never know you like this again.

"Do you remember the time I tripped on the bus when we were getting off."

"What? What time? When?"

"We were just coming back from class and we were getting off at your stop across from the Cherry Street bar and I tripped in the aisle and you started laughing, and I laughed, and then I said something to you. Do you remember what I said?"

"What was it?"

"I said I wouldn't regret this. That whatever happened between us and because of us, I wouldn't regret it."

You lay back then and pulled the covers above your breasts and said, "Let's go get some ice cream," and though it was about the last thing I wanted on that cold, cold night, we stumbled outside into the bitter chill, feeling foolish because the town was closed for winter. We drifted around for a few blocks until we were saved by a single sign, "Homemade ice cream," shining like a song in the wind, howling now, and us young enough to think the universe was telling us something about ourselves, giving us this moment when really it was just two people stumbling around in the cold looking for ice cream. Inside the parlor, it was warm and we got our cones—Rocky Road for me and something called Banana Cherry-Red Raspberry for you. We sat eating, our hands touching beneath the table, maybe our most intimate moment.

You said then you were tired of slumming, that last word like a slap.

"Like this," I said. "With me?"

"Oh, Stewart, you know what I mean."

And I remembered again then how your father was a surgeon, and how I never spoke of mine, the postman, and I nodded and smiled and said nothing.

You wanted to give something back. "I'm thinking of interning in Africa," you said.

I nodded, remembering how your old boyfriend studied German and hung out with the squatters who stole credit card receipts from trashcans and threw red paint on mink coats.

"Cool," I said finally. "That's really cool."

THE NEXT MORNING THE terrorist attack, the first one, was all over the papers. You were thrilled and I felt sick, and it was, in some sense, the real beginning of the end, but we didn't know anything about that then. It wasn't a small story, but it felt like one, nothing like when it happened that second time and the whole world stopped and pivoted on a dime.

"Look at that?" I said.

It was in a machine, across the street from our hotel. You bent down and read the headline without buying the paper.

"Terrorists Bomb World Trade Center," the headline read.

You said something snappy and quick, something about your old anarchist boyfriend, your squatter friends. We all felt like replacements, like no one's sons, no one's daughters, and it seemed, right then, like more of the same, we'd lived through Reagan and Bush I, and this was just another shitty thing happening out there in the world beyond us, nothing to do with the rubbery texture of our lives, certainly nothing to do with the salt in the air, the rumble in our stomachs, our urgent need for pancakes. The wind off the water pushed us along, and the town, mostly empty, felt blue, but, eventually, we found a diner with one old-woman waitress, and we sat down and ordered our breakfasts. It wasn't until you said something about how happy that bomb made you, though I certainly don't think you used that word, that I understood Rita was probably right. Right about never coming here with me, right about you, and it was in that moment, waiting for our food, waiting to be fed, that I felt how lonely it was living inside yourself, how foolish and empty that place can be—and how, even though I felt I'd die if I didn't get up and away from you, I knew a part of me was already dead, so I stayed right where I was—next to you, among the bread trucks, terrorists, and spies.

"Remember," you began, before I reached out and touched your lips with my finger.

WHITEOUT

I PARKED MY WHITE Fox in front of my father's pink house in the suburbs and stumbled inside to catch Dad rising dewy-eyed from his red E-Z-Boy ready to claim me with a rare embrace. I was back in Philly, fresh from Montana, where I'd gone to become a writer, not in any clichéd way, but authentically, by living among the people, à la Whitman and Kerouac, as I once told my good friend Gabe I would. (And Gabe, as was his way, had laughed uproariously, called me naïve, singing, "What people, Stewart? Exactly what people?") Somehow, I'd made it home alive after driving nearly 3,000 miles in my beat-to-shit 1979 Audi Fox, the last 250 miles, a death-defying slide across the snow-slicked Pennsylvania Turnpike. In the middle of the storm, my driver-side wiper blade had quit, leaving me stranded somewhere outside of Harrisburg, but my cash was so low I couldn't afford to stop and bunk down at a hotel for the night. Instead, I'd called Dad, and he'd told me I'd have to go to a hardware store and *replace* the rubber part of the wiper blade. Shivering at a rest stop's payphone, this news left me nearly speechless with wonder. *Replace the blade?*

"It doesn't last forever," Dad explained

That same year during Thanksgiving Break, I'd flown to LA to visit Gabe and his screenwriting buddies, all laboring assiduously at USC film school trying to become the next Quentin Tarantino, this a few years after the previous batch of students had all labored assiduously to become the next Martin Scorsese. I think now of the words and phrases out West—whiteout, pass, you bet—and all those magical place names: Bitterroot, Blackfoot, Victor, Three Forks, Yaak, Havre, Libby, Lolo, Whitefish. I felt protected by such names, loved even. Visiting Gabe, I'd driven from Missoula to Spokane in the middle of the night to catch a red-eye to LA. The roads that night were mostly deserted, and the snow had started somewhere outside of Coeur d'Alene, leaving me alone to navigate the one hundred and seventy-nine brain-screaming miles across two mountain passes. The closest feeling was terror, a slippery, pure feeling that at any moment the Audi could quit, would quit, and I'd be stranded on the side of the road in the middle of the night waiting until someone happened along and decided to save my sorry ass. If they even saw me, that is, as the white car, and me in it, had just about disappeared in the near-whiteout conditions. I was so tense and sure that I was going to die that I yanked at myself like a crazed monkey as I drove, jerking off on the long straight-aways between the passes, coming gloriously and feeling, finally, a little bit like my hero, Whitman.

BUT THAT WAS NOVEMBER. This was December, and now I was home, greeting my father. Our hug done, Dad led me into the kitchen, pulled half a hoagie from the fridge and poured me a tall glass of Pepsi-Cola, the sound of the soda popping and fizzing over the ice releasing my entire boyhood into the air. Home. I was home.

"So Dad. How's it going? What's been going on around here?"

"Same old thing," my father said, his big Jimmy Durante nose hanging out in front of him like a piece of evidence. "I fall asleep in front of the television every night."

He was old, close to eighty, and I didn't know how I'd

survive his loss—couldn't have imagined that at his funeral, as others dropped roses, I'd have the need to flatten my hand against his bronze casket blazing in the August sun to measure such steel with the flesh of my palm.

As I ate my hoagie at the kitchen table, the neighbor's dog woofed and howled, while Dad grimaced and scratched at the back of his hand. The neighbor kept the dog tied to a post twenty-four/seven, offering the animal only the circumference of a three-foot leash to shit, eat, sleep—and, of course, the dog never shut up because of it, just barked incessantly, nearly driving my old man insane. At first my father had simply pitched pebbles into the neighbor's yard, aiming at the dirt in front of the animal, hoping to scare the dog into silence. He wouldn't call the police, though, because from where Dad hailed you didn't call the cops on your neighbors unless there was theft or death, but when he asked the neighbor to quiet the dog, to simply let it off its leash for a few hours a day, they ignored him, so Dad finally phoned the SPCA. Nothing changed, though, and my father grew accustomed to the noise, and years later, when the owner of the dog was murdered in Chester at a check-cashing place he owned, my Dad sent a Mass card, telling me he'd always felt bad about calling the SPCA.

At the kitchen table, I tried to explain Montana to my father: "The people are hard to describe. They're not angry for one thing. I mean they say "hi," when you pass them on the street. It's weird being around so many friendly people."

My father, a West Philly kid, flashed a grin. He understood. In Philly, friendly strangers usually wanted your money, or maybe something more. Wise guys, he called them. Dad didn't play that game. He was raised during the Great Depression. His father was a union man, but

Dad was never exactly one way or the other about almost anything. Instead, he was a man who sought the middle ground on most every topic, except maybe work, the need to get up every day and go to work. It's the thing he taught me the most.

Earlier that week, from the road, I'd sent him a card with a Charlie Russell reproduction on its front, some cowboy in chaps with a drippy handlebar moustache. It laid now on the kitchen table, next to his coffee cup, and I knew he'd sat with his coffee and brooded over my card, worrying about my long trip. I could see him there, his love as palpable as a stone. What I'd written wasn't much, "Dear Dad, the road is great. I'm so happy traveling all day, observing the world passing at 65 MPH. Jill is great too. She says hi." Reading it, my bad handwriting sprang up at me like an embarrassing photograph and my message sounded too sappy, too light to match the seriousness of my father's concern. Was I drunk when I wrote it? Probably. One good thing, though, was I'd written that I would be home around the twentieth, and today, magically, was Dec. 20. I'd done something right, so I looked into my father's eyes then, and he saw me and smiled. I smiled back. I don't think I ever felt his love the way I felt it that night, my first night home from Montana.

A COUPLE OF DAYS later, at my sister's annual Christmas Eve party, some neighbor guy (whose son, a few years later, would die tragically in one of those impossibly stupid teenager car accidents—the son losing control of his car as he took rises on the road at 70 MPH just to get airborne for a few precious seconds of fun only, in the end, to crash into a tree) had asked about the trees in Montana, if there were any other kinds besides pines. I laughed, thinking this was his idea of a joke, and told him that where I lived in the Rattlesnake Creek Apartments black bears regularly trotted down from the mountains to pillage among the dumpsters along my complex. He sort of smiled, shook his head, and walked away. After his son's accident, I saw this man at another one of my sister's Christmas Eve bashes. His shoulders sagged, he shuffled—the life had been drained from him, and I wanted to remind him how he had asked me about trees that one night and how I had talked instead of bears, but this no longer seemed appropriate because his son was dead and I was no longer young.

Two NIGHTS LATER, MY sister's party in the books, my brother, his wife, and their three kids were in town, and all six of us were squeezed into my father's squat little ranch house, so I headed into the city. I was thinking of Woody's, a gay bar at 13th and Locust, maybe looking for Darrell, a friend whose penis I'd placed in my mouth last April on the anniversary of my mother's death. I'd liked the symmetry of that, the sucking and the death—liked too how Darrell had offered me vodka and pot, and liked, mostly, how with guys you didn't have to pretend, how sometimes all you wanted was your dick sucked, a desire somehow (sort of) sated by sucking someone else's dick.

Darrell, though, wasn't around that night, so I settled into a seat at the bar, not ready to head back to Boothwyn just yet. The lighting in the bar was bad, and the smell of cologne and smoke smothered everything, but what thrilled me was the way the men looked at each other, the way they looked at me, how quickly and openly desire was exchanged, like coins at an arcade. I'd spent a lifetime unlearning these looks, so to have men look at me like that, and to look that way myself, freed me. I especially liked the way the transvestite at the end of the bar looked my way, her eyes wide and provocative with just a hint of laughter—along with something else, something deeper, a sadness that drew me in. He was a beautiful woman with a slender neck and the jaw of a man. I knew I could love such a person, a person like me, like my father, a person caught squarely in the middle, forever. She smiled. I smiled right back, and in the next moment she was sitting next to me, her menthol breath all over me.

"Hey, baby. You look like you lost something," she said.

"Nope, I'm cool," I laughed. "I'm just hanging out."

"You sure? Why you look so sad?"

"Sad? I'm so far from sad. I'm the happiest man alive. I'm from Montana."

"Montana? Listen to you," she said. "You're funny, aren't you. Are you a funny guy?"

"Maybe. I don't know. It depends who listens."

"I get you," she said, reaching for my lighter on the bar. She had thick blue veins on the back of her hands. "I'm just so glad you're not sad because there's no reason to be sad, only sad people should be sad, right? And who cares about those saddies?"

"Not me," I said, draining my drink and grinning some more.

"What's your name, honey?" she asked.

"William," I said. "William Fox."

She laughed, realized I was lying, I guess, and told me to call her Tina. She had luscious tits, this Tina, and her nipples stood erect beneath the soft fabric of her dress. Her mouth was full and pretty. I wanted her. The bulge beneath her purse on her lap didn't matter at all. We chatted on, waiting for the inevitable exit together. She finally brought it up.

"So what are you thinking? You want to go somewhere?"

"Sure. Why not? Where? Now?"

"Now? Listen to you. Of course now."

"Where?"

"Your place."

"OK," I said, even though, and maybe because, my place was nearly two thousand miles away in Montana.

"Let me just go to the little girls' room and I'll be right back," she said.

She got up, and I waited for nothing and everything, eyeing myself in the mirror behind the bar when Darrell suddenly appeared from nowhere, eyes blazing.

"What the hell are you doing?" he asked. "Do you know she'll beat your ass and take your wallet, after she takes what else you want to give her. Jesus, boy, what are you doing here?"

I smiled, said nothing. It was good to be home.

"Aren't you supposed to be in Montana?"

"I was looking for you."

He shook his head and frowned. "I thought you were in Montana."

"I was. I am."

He was still frowning, "Just don't go anywhere with her. OK? Don't be an idiot."

Though my father preferred the word *goof*, this sounded exactly like a piece of advice Dad would have given me, and it was one of the reasons I liked Darrell—the blunt way he spoke, the words he used. I knew him from the Frog where we both had worked as waiters before I'd left for Montana.

And I can't mention the Frog, without mentioned how when I'd told the folks there that I was leaving for Montana to study writing, I don't think many people believed me.

Montana sounded like a story you might tell before disappearing into a crack house in Fishtown. I'm sure people remembered the time I told everyone I'd been awarded a $50,000 artist's grant from the Pew Charitable Trust. I thought it was true at the time because a man named Stewart Simmons was listed among the winners, but unfortunately there was another Stewart Simmons in town, another writer, a famous one, or at least published and all, a jazz critic to boot—and it was this guy who'd won the grant, not me, but for a few days I'd been him, the winner, this other Stewart Simmons. It felt great. People bought me drinks. They listened when I spoke. When I discovered the mix-up and told people the truth, it seemed to convince the crowd at the Frog of something that they already suspected about me, and we all went back to stealing the good vodka, the fine wines, and having our parties, fucking one another when the need arose, before I did finally disappear into Montana.

At the bar, Darrell was still waiting at my shoulder. Only an hour ago, before Woody's, I'd sat in a strip bar, building courage and getting drunk, as I stared forlornly into the vagina of an average-looking white girl from South Philly. Now, I had what I came for—Darrell, a big man, squat, with football shoulders. The only thing remotely feminine about him was his voice, which he projected girlishly at times, but at other times delivered in a mellow Barry-White kind of way that made my insides go all squishy. I'd loved him, and in a real way, but we had fooled around only a couple times before I'd left for Montana, and, though, I hadn't really thought about him since leaving, here he was, saving me.

"Let's get out of here," Darrell said, finally, touching my arm at the elbow, right below the bicep. "Back to my place. Before she comes back from the bathroom."

"Sounds like a plan. I can drive. I have a car."

"You have a car?" Darrell said, widening his eyes in mock wonder. "Wow, what kind?"

"An Audi."

He smiled his smooth white smile. Darrell loved money. He fashioned himself a harlot, a vixen, a trashy gay minx, but I knew, really, he was exactly like me, a guy too smart for his circumstances, a man trapped in his own life, someone determined to play out every permutation just to see what it felt like, to see where it might lead.

"I always knew you had money."

"Don't get excited, Darrell. It's an old car."

"Doesn't matter. Money is money."

When he saw the car he just laughed, reminding me of that morning he had stayed over and my father had showed up early to help me move. That night, we drove back to his place, a loft at Broad and Washington, to discover his husband wasn't home, and I kneeled in front of him in his kitchen and took his fat dick into my mouth, realizing at that moment this was exactly what I wanted, what I had driven all those miles to get—this penis in my mouth. In Montana, despite the beauty, I was bored because the men were men and everyone was white, even the Indians. Only the women were interesting because many knew how to hunt, change a car's oil, and fix the plumbing. There was no one like Darrell, someone mixed up and free. We went into his bedroom where thick velvet drapes covered the windows, like curtains on a stage, and in bed I put Darrell in my mouth again, but he was soft now, and I teased him a bit until I saw something flare in his eyes. I told him then I wanted him inside me, though I couldn't imagine that. He kneeled between me and spread my legs with his shoulders, touching my anus with one wet finger. It hurt. I squirmed away closed my legs, and he stopped and began rubbing his cock over my chest as he stared off. So this is the way it works, I thought. I was drunk and curious and horny in that order. It went on for a while, this stroking, this staring off, until he came on my stomach, the sticky warmth there wonderful, like I'd won a prize. He fetched a towel and some water to wipe my belly clean, the way a mother might wipe her baby. Afterwards, we slept.

In the morning, we shared half a joint before I dropped him off at work and drove home to my father's. And I would see Darrell only once more, two years later, at an art house cinema downtown while I was home again visiting the old man. He was with someone else, another white guy, another me. They were laughing and looked happy. I smiled along with them, waiting for Darrell to turn and recognize me, but, of course, it was too late for anything like that. I'd morphed, strangely enough, into a sportswriter and gone fat. Darrell didn't even see me. That old me was long gone.

WHEN I ARRIVED BACK at my father's house from Darrell's place, my brother, his lovely wife, their three fuzzy-headed kids—Matt, Mark, and Malcolm—and my father, were all eating breakfast in Dad's bread-box shaped kitchen. The smell of scrapple and eggs filled the kitchen, and the fluorescent light was just awful enough to save me. I grunted a greeting, wondering exactly what I smelled like beneath the smell of that scrapple, before I slumped downstairs to sleep for a few hours in my old bedroom in the basement, the same basement where as a boy I would wake after a hard rain to find water an inch-deep on the floor. I awoke on those mornings as if on a raft, as if on a journey, and after sleeping for a few hours that morning at Dad's, I awoke to the smell of my father's meatloaf, the recipe for which I'd find years later while boxing up his things after he'd died. The recipe was a dish my mother used to cook. It came from her mother. My wife cooks it now. It's utterly delicious:

> 1 lb of ground beef
> ½ cup of bread crumbs
> 1 large egg
> ½ teaspoon each of garlic powder, basil, oregano, and thyme
> ½ onion finely chopped
> 16-ounce can of tomato sauce
> salt to taste.

Today, when I come across this recipe, written in my dad's florid handwriting and stuffed in my wife's recipe book, I read it again and again, searching for some lost ingredient, some mysterious way as to how it all fits together.

MONTANA

YOU WERE ALL SILK lace, polite talk, and money, a daughter of professors, a mystery to a working guy like me, but we found each other because we both wanted to slut it up in Montana, to drink and dance in bars among cowboys, loggers, and magicians, to drive those long forever roads beneath the skin of the sky stretching out in front of us like an invitation to the rest of our lives. In Montana, it felt like anything could happen, and it usually did. I bought an ancient Audi Fox, a white one, for $900 from a girl who lived in a condo across the street from Dick Hugo's grave, and when that first weekend came, a balmy Saturday in October, we headed to Yaak with the windows rolled down. Some writer or other had wintered there and written about it, which was enough for us. On the way to Yaak, we stopped in Libby, an old mining town where half the population was dying of asbestos poisoning and the other half just didn't give a damn. We found a bar, of course. We always found a bar.

Inside, sitting next to a man who claimed to jockey horses in California during the summer, we listened, believing everything, as he talked on about horse tranquilizers, illegal bets, and steak dinners at midnight. Montanans didn't care much for Californians so anyone in Montana claiming to be from California was probably from California. Not that we cared. We just wanted a story, so we simply nodded and grinned, dropping shots of tomato juice into our draft beers as he told his tales. I wanted him to get up so I could see if he were short enough to be a jockey, and to see if he wore cowboy boots. I knew the details would be important.

"Which way to Yaak?" I asked him when he was done talking.

"I could drive you there," he said, squinting at me as you leaned against my shoulder, laughing.

"No, we're cool," I said.

Youth is like a drug, Fitzgerald said, and we were feeling it, young and foolish, the kind of people we don't recognize today, don't understand—like those kids we saw just yesterday leaving the coffee shop only to stand in front of the shop's windows kissing for minutes before they climbed into their purple van and drove away. Why stand there kissing like that? Why not just drive off together and get on with it? We looked away and got back to our business (whatever that was), trying to ignore that tickle beneath our skin, our past lives scratching to get out

When we arrived, Yaak was one paved street, two bars, and a post office. It was just after ten, no hotel in sight, no gas station, even, and Libby was sixty-eight miles behind us, but we didn't care. We skipped into the bar to find it packed, the jukebox miraculously screaming the Violet Fems—*Big hands you're the one*—and a man dressed head-to-toe in calfskin, a David Crockett knife attached to his leather belt. He danced a little jig in the middle of the floor littered with sawdust and peanut shells. We looked at each other with ravenous wonder, delighted and in love.

"This is like a dream," I shouted to you over the music.

"What? I can't hear you?"

"Don't wake me up," I said, shaking my head.

You smiled. "I won't."

What I want to say is that in Montana, you and I laughed and drank and danced and fucked in a way that led us to believe that this was our life—booze, magic, and road trips—that this was all we needed. Our lives bled beauty, and everywhere we looked, some draw-dropping spectacle popped up before us as if our eyes were what gave this mountain, this river, its very life. I've never been happier. Once, we pulled over near Polson, right before the lake, and climbed into the back of your pickup (Montana a place where even women drove pickups) and fucked furiously beneath the stars in the bed of your truck, the cars shuddering past, you breathing heavily into my ear. I wondered what it looked like to you, the bee-stung sky above, and me deep inside, as deep as I could go and with everything I had.

See, Montana was just a silly little song we couldn't get out of our heads, but at that moment, in Yaak, right after we saw the calfskin man doing his jig, it felt as if we'd found the nectar, the secret for which others spend a lifetime searching. A few minutes later, you asked for the car key to retrieve a pack of smokes, and a few minutes after that, you came back in tears, your fingers red raw. You were sobbing, trying to explain how you'd broken off the key trying to open the trunk. "I'm so sorry," you said. "We're stranded. I'm such a fucking idiot."

But it was OK. I held your fingers in my hands and blew on them, telling you the broken key wasn't for the engine—the car was old enough to have separate keys for the ignition and the trunk. You laughed, and we kissed and drank our last shots, and when the bar closed, the fun done, we cruised like innocents, back to Libby, back to reality. We passed countless little white crosses marking the spots where people had died in accidents, but it felt like nothing could touch us, not yet. We weren't destined to be some sad newspaper story forever linked to one of those melancholy mushroom crosses. We knew we were better than that (we had chains and an emergency blanket in the trunk!) or maybe just luckier, but somehow, we made it those sixty-eight miles to Libby, a hotel, and then all the way to here, Lincoln, Nebraska, our little life here today, the shared tender secrets of our children, our dreams all dreamt up.

I only wonder if it's enough.

RATTLESNAKE CREEK APARTMENTS

MY FATHER SAID HE wasn't going to walk into that crumbling Victorian in North Philly only to have someone knock him on the head with a claw hammer and take his cash. Not my old man. Not for a cat, he said. It was my cat in the care of a girl I'd once dated. Sarah was the girl, Reed the cat. I'd left Reed with Sarah before I left Philly for Montana to begin a new life. That was the plan anyway, before Sarah phoned one morning to say she couldn't care for the cat anymore, a skittish, long-haired Angora, so I'd have to send someone to pick up the animal. Hence Dad. This was my life in those days, a new address every six months, a new plan, new hopes, new dreams, but Montana felt like the real deal. Before, I'd measured my moves in blocks, but now there were two thousand miles between me and anything and anyone that I'd even known or loved.

Just yesterday morning, when I took my coffee to the front patio I heard a racket coming from a dumpster I shared with the three other units at the Rattlesnake Creek Apartments. In the blur of morning I thought it was a homeless person, but this was Montana, I remembered, so I thought raccoon, a pair of them, before I witnessed the shaggy hump of a black bear lift itself from the steel container and lumber across the road toward Mount Jumbo, turning to eye me for a hard second before disappearing into the tree line. I stood there breathless, clenching my ass cheeks, trying not to shit my pants.

I'd hooked up with Sarah after one of the last parties I'd

worked at the Frog, a wedding reception for 200 held on a sprawling estate in Chadds Ford, the heart of Wyeth country, where N.C. and Andrew had painted their brooding landscapes, fatted pigs, and stern, lovely nudes. The wedding grounds included long sloping Gatsby-like lawns where the guests had mingled during the cocktail hour, politely laughing and chatting as we served them gourmet miniature meatballs, smoked salmon on crackers and pan-seared tuna on sticks. We worked under a harsh June sun, tugging at the collars of our polyester tuxedoes as we weaved among the guests in their linen clothes, feeling superior to their stiff looks and mannered ways, their lotioned and cologned skin—what we assumed they had to do to earn and keep their money. Between courses we swilled good vodka behind the garages and cooled ourselves with the hoses there, bitching and moaning, telling off-color jokes about the discrete charms of the bourgeois, and when it was over, ten hours later, I was somehow seriously sucking face with Sarah in the back seat of a cab.

When the cab had pulled up at my one-bedroom apartment above a tax accountant's office in South Philly, Sarah had climbed out and followed me upstairs before she plopped down on her knees in my bedroom, unzipped me, and took me into her mouth. It was a breathless moment, and coming as it did after such a long, dumb, alcohol-soaked day of brutal work and monkey-suit humiliation, it felt like an offering, an epiphany of sorts, something you might build a life upon—or at least ride for a few salty weeks. I brushed Sarah's hair with my fingertips, hair as soft as her mouth, surprisingly so, because she kept it short, spiked, and dyed a harsh white, the color of paper.

"Does that feel good?" she said coming up to my mouth at exactly the wrong time, her breath all cock and alcohol.

"So good," I said before we clumsily clicked teeth and I fell backward, nicking my head against the wall.

I cursed. She laughed, and I touched the back of my head, bringing my fingers inches from my eyes so I could see the dark dab of blood, smell its milky richness.

Now, Dad was on phone telling me he wasn't going to walk into that damn house and have someone knock him on the head with a claw hammer.

"You should have seen the place," he explained. "Inside the front door looked like a tunnel, long and dark, and I could hear voices laughing way back like it was a party or something. One o'clock on a Wednesday and it sounded like a weekend."

"Well, Dad, you know caterers have odd hours."

As did grad students because at the Rattlesnake it was almost one and I was still lounging on my futon bed with Jill—the zenith of my life and what I felt mostly was hungover, day after day.

"Yeah, well, I didn't know these people from Adam, so if I go in there and someone whacks me on the head, I'm done," he said. "I stayed right where I was."

"Dad, c'mon, that's ridiculous—no one would do that," I said, though, honestly, it sounded exactly like something someone might do in Philly—one of the reasons I'd fled the place.

"How's Reed?" I asked.

"He's good. You'll see him soon enough. I just got him on the plane. He should be there in a few hours."

Jill, my lazy, good-hearted new girl, stirred beside me, rubbing the sleep from her eyes and asking the time. I smiled at her, shrugged. We spent our nights riding waves of alcohol, cigarettes, and big talk. Our program was considered elite, a top-of-the-line MFA, Grade-A beef. Many of my fellow students had graduated from the best schools, Brown, Swarthmore, Oberlin, and they were as sure of their future successes as the next sunrise—once they got serious about their lives, of course. But for now it was mostly about having a good time. Last night had been pool hall beer and whiskey until 2:00 a.m., a house party afterward, then huckleberry pancakes and coffee at 4:00 at the Oxford on Higgins, all under the brooding eyes of Missoula's toast-colored mountains and its long, glorious sky speckled with stars. It'd started snowing moments before we'd ducked into the diner for our pancakes—and the lovely, fat flakes had served as a type of punctuation to the evening's fun. We giggled like toddlers, sticking out our tongues to catch the frozen pearls. Eric, a Harvard man, had fallen then and skinned his knee. "Fuck," he squealed, getting up and hobbling around. "Fuck, fuck, fuck."

In Philly, when Sarah had fallen to her knees, Chad, a fattish white guy we worked with at the Frog, a guy I didn't really know nor like, but with whom, for some reason, I'd been spending a lot of time, had drifted through my mind like smoke. The last time we'd hung out, Chad had told me Sarah had sauntered up to him at the tail-end of a dinner and cocktails for seventy-five bank executives at the Franklin Institute and whispered, "I want to suck your cock."

I didn't really believe Chad until Sarah had dropped to her knees before me, and when she did so, I reconsidered all his stories, like how he'd once said he'd screwed two $1000 prostitutes in Atlantic City in one night and how one of the women's underwear had matched his girlfriend's exactly, "Christian Dior, pink, the kind I like." Chad was mostly an asshole, but in those days I was drawn to the type—cynics, misanthropes, liars, I think, because I felt their rudeness, their lack of constraint might hold some key into the heart of things, some understanding of how the world actually worked, and how, ultimately, to get past the things that could swallow a life whole—heartbreak, regret, debt. I wondered too what was moving around inside of Sarah—waiting to be born, because despite all this cock sucking, Sarah dated girls mostly, but here she was offering herself up like some Biblical whore. I knew the feeling, and had done some of the same things with Darrell, and while she was still on her knees before me, I thought I might just live this way forever, but then she'd stopped doing what she was doing and stood up to ask how much I liked it—a question that cut the life out of the moment because it was not about liking anything. I dreaded almost everything I did, and knew I had to escape Philly soon if I hoped to survive.

ON THE PHONE THAT morning in Montana, Dad explained how he'd managed to get Reed onto the plane, telling a long involved story of how he'd almost given up because the cat wouldn't come out from hiding (he was a shy cat), but then at the last moment Reed had appeared and Dad had managed to slip the tranquilizer into his food and hustle him into his cage and then to the airport.

"He wasn't too happy," Dad said.

"No crap," I said.

Everyone had their story. My dad had his. Me, I had just a glimmer of a clue.

After hanging up the phone with Dad, the long groan of the train whistled up from the valley while Jill and I lolled out of bed. I put on my blue kimono robe, made coffee, and started cracking eggs over a hot skillet. Over easy, the way Jill liked them. She followed me into the kitchen, leaned against the sink and yawned, half watching me cook, half watching a woman plunking the last of the tomatoes from the stalks in the garden behind our apartment. It was nearly October. Up on the mountains, the ash trees were turning yellow. Winter would be here soon, my first Montana winter. I had no clue.

This garden belonged to a young couple who lived in a blue house badly in need of a new coat of paint. They had this little baby, and that morning the woman had the infant in what looked to be a potato sack tied around the front of her as she collected the last of her tomatoes. She had a rope of blonde hair hanging down her back and was stuffing the fruit down into the sack holding the child, and I was thinking about shit. The shit maybe leaking from the diapered infant, the shit that helped grow those tomatoes, the shit some people made of their lives. Jill poured herself a cup of coffee and asked about Sarah, why she had my cat in the first place. I mumbled something about her love of animals, her friendly nature, but I didn't want to talk about Sarah. I wanted to talk about the truck.

"What do you think her name is?" Jill asked, sipping her coffee and nodding at the woman in the garden.

"I have no idea. Rain, Patricia, Desdemona, Summer. A rose is a rose is a rose. What's the difference?" I said, my head feeling like a fight.

"Someone's mister grumpy today," Jill said, poking at my belly.

Along with the baby, the shack house, and the garden, the couple had a rusty green pickup that the man had to crank five, six, seven times each morning to turn it over. I would hear him most days when I'd wake up for a few moments and blink in the dark, thinking how cold it must be out there, how much colder it was going to get, before

I turned over and burrowed deeper into the blankets. Last week, I'd watched him leave for work while we were still up drinking from the night before. I couldn't imagine his life. It seemed so perfectly contained, yet dead, and it scared the hell out of me for reasons I did not fully understand.

Jill watched the mother and baby, cooing about how perfect their life seemed, though all I could think about was the man working that truck in the dark until it finally shuddered to life. He usually went to work in dirty jeans and a Carhartt jacket, and I guessed whatever he did wasn't easy. My own father had worked at the U.S. Post Office for forty years. He left for work each morning before I was out of bed to catch the 5:00 a.m. express to 30th Street, but on some mornings I'd hear him in the shower. The squeak of the faucet, the dull thud of the water drumming the tub and his naked back. He never sang, but sometimes hummed softly, so softly so as not to wake us. The first time I heard it I thought it was something else—a dream, a TV show, the urgent hiss of burglars.

"Are you still drunk?" Jill asked.

"No. I don't think so," I said, managing a smile. "I just have no idea what her name is."

Jill smiled back. "Of course you don't. Have you ever even talked to them?"

"I'm from Philly, we don't talk to our neighbors."

"Oh, c'mon, just look at her. Doesn't she look happy? They have the perfect life."

"Do you hear the truck every morning?" I said, coming around to Jill and circling her with my arms, my cock instantly hard against her ass as we watched the woman with her baby in front of her.

"What truck?" Jill asked, pushing back against me. "I never hear a truck."

•

A YEAR LATER, JILL showed up at the Rattlesnake on the wrong side of midnight. She was in tears, kicking at my front door, screaming. We were done by then (I'd grown bored and restless), and I'd purchased a big, new bed and in it was Jessica, a native Montanan, cat-eyed and serious, so serious she believed she was the reincarnation of Ann Boleyn—too serious, really. She drove me wild, though, and if I'd the guts and the smarts to have stayed with her I might have been the happiest, or dead, or at least busy enough with her craziness not to dwell so far inside of things, closest to the sadness. During our first night together, she'd told me all kinds of her secrets—what she liked best: the smell of rain, medieval history, modern dance, and sex—all of it, anal, oral, the works. She told me how she'd once fucked a friend of hers just because she liked the girl's dress.

"I mean, I really liked that dress," she said, laughing. "And once I slept with her I knew I could just borrow it."

"You mean you couldn't just borrow it without sleeping with her?"

She laughed some more. "I could have, I guess, but it was way more fun my way."

Jessica, from Arlee, was nineteen, maybe twenty, an undergrad; I was pushing thirty—a dangerous equation, but she called me "Stewart," in a way no one had before or since, and her desire electrified me—the first time we made love she thrashed and moaned so much I thought she was either having a seizure or trying to communicate with her god, but she had simply, I learned later, had an orgasm, or two, and had soaked the sheets on my new bed with her girl juice. I had no idea.

"Is that her? Your old girlfriend? Does she hate me?" Jessica asked the night Jill showed up at the Rattlesnake to

bang on my door. Jessica was sitting up in bed now, something like irony or pity or maybe just innocence filling her
face as Jill began kicking hard at the door.

"SHHH," I said.

I went to the door in that silly kimono, a relic from my
aborted trip to Japan—the first place I'd gone to begin
again, telling Jess to stay put, give me one minute.

I told a very drunk Jill that she would have to go home.
"Is she in there? She's in there, isn't she? I can't believe
you're fucking a freshman."

"She's a sophomore," I said.

"But why don't you fuck me?"

She came up to me and put her hands on my chest,
saying more of the same. It was not good. Eventually, she
left and I went back to bed, to Jessica.

"I'm so sorry," Jessica said, touching my eyelids in the
dark with the tips of her fingers before kissing me there. "I
feel so sorry for her."

"Go to sleep," I said. "She's just wasted. She'll feel better
tomorrow."

She reached down touched my soft cock. Stopped.

"This feels like a dream," she said.

"My cock feels like a dream?"

She laughed and said, "Yeah, I wish I had a cock."

THE MORNING SARAH HAD phoned from Philly and told
me she couldn't take care of Reed anymore, I said fine, I
understood—he was a temperamental cat, but I think she'd
expected more from me, not an uncommon complaint, and
that somehow Reed would have kept us connected, though
we'd never been connected in any real way in the first place.
Back then, I didn't understand what people needed from
me, what I offered. What I did know, and what I never

tired of telling anyone, especially if they were buying the next round, was that until the fifteenth century, romantic love didn't even exist as a concept.

"In the West," Jill said, showing off her Northwestern education. "In Asia, the concept stretches back at least a thousand years."

"Yeah, well. Missoula ain't Tokyo," I said.

"Whatever, Romeo, that's just something you read in a book or heard in a class anyway."

"Yeah, so?"

"Well, duh, everyone wants someone," Jill said. "That's how the heart works."

"Everyone?"

"Everyone I know."

"Not me," I said, lying.

The one I'd wanted most was Fiona, but she didn't want me. I met her shortly after the aborted trip to Japan, a few years before I left for Montana. I loved her because of her breasts, which were lovely and full of stories. The first time I touched them she said, "I don't know if I want to sleep with you or see you again," and I said, "Why not both?" and she had looked at me as if I'd just won the lotto, which I'd felt I had, and we were together that night and a few glorious more. The second time I touched her breasts, she told me her brother was the first person to make her come, by rubbing her breasts. "Like this," she said showing me how. "It was just a game we played as kids," she told me. "But after that, we knew we had to stop." The third time I touched her breasts she said she loved me and invited me to Colorado, where I met the brother and his magical hands. I also met her mother, who, in the middle of a light rain drizzle as we sat inside their sprawling house in the mountains just outside of Denver said it wasn't raining and when I said, "Yes, it is," she said, "No it isn't," and I realized it could go on like that forever, but wouldn't and didn't. Later that same week, Fiona and I drove to Colorado Springs, and we took a soak in a hot spring, bubbles tickling our chins, hugging while she slipped me stiff from my suit, wrapped her legs around me, and sliding me right up inside her in the middle of a pool full of people. I sighed a ridiculously long sigh, the most pleasure I'd ever known.

"SHHHHH," she said.

Later, in her parent's sparkling Audi on the way back to Denver, I told Fiona I didn't think there was a way to get old without giving up.

"Giving up what?" she asked.

"I don't know exactly, something important, essential—your true self, I guess—as corny as that sounds. I mean did you see those people in the hot springs? The men looked pregnant, the women were zombies. The fucking kids."

"People see what they want to see," she said. "And I thought that was a pretty good fuck."

THAT MORNING, JILL AND I sat forking our eggs, which I'd salted too much, finishing our coffee, waiting for Reed to make his way across the country in the bottom of a plane. My mouth had begun loosening up, but it still tasted like ash and my liver felt bruised, my throat burned. I wondered how many more mornings I would sacrifice like this—hung-over and drunk, hung-over and drunk, again and again.

"You've never really heard that dude grinding his truck in the morning?" I asked Jill again. For some reason, I wanted to make this a thing.

"No. Why? What do you think he does?" she asked.

"Who knows? I have no idea what people do in this

town, how people live here, but the fucking truck is crazy."
The couple was often in their yard. We weren't. In a way,
I didn't really care about them, but Jill couldn't stop talking
about them. They seemed poor, but happy, a little aloof, like
most hippies I knew, and like most native Montanans, for
that matter. I thought of myself as a hippie, to be honest,
but never a Montanan. So did Jill. I suppose that's why we
talked so much about them in those days—maybe we saw
our future selves, maybe we saw our little daughter—who,
by the way, is a native Montanan, but isn't aloof. That's
one reason, I suppose, we paid them so much mind, but
that doesn't sound exactly right either. There was something else there too, something fleeting and hard to place,
something in the grind of that truck and how easy it was
to burrow down into my blankets and go back to sleep, to
forget. It felt as if choices were being made but the param-
eters were unclear, unexplained, the alternatives murky as
a muddy pond you might stumble upon as a child at play,
deep in the woods. I knew my education was meant to save
me from this man's fate, but I didn't really believe that, and
wasn't certain he needed saving.

WHEN REED FINALLY ARRIVED he was bathed in his own
feces—shit covered the bottom of his cage, as well as his
long angora coat. I'm sure he'd shat shortly after Dad had
stuffed him into the cage that morning and then had stewed
in it for a good two-thousand miles, the two long transfers
in Minnesota and Utah. They kept him down below with
the rest of the luggage where the noise, most likely, had pet-
rified him. Or maybe, I hoped, the pill my father had given
Reed worked, maybe he'd slept most of the way. Whatever
had happened to him, he was wild-looking and weak when
he arrived, and I felt awful at having put him through all

that just so he could live with the likes of me. In the airport, after picking up his cage, I found a quiet part of the terminal and pulled him free of the cage, shit and all, and held him close, talking low and soothing into his ear.

Jill scuttled up beside me, saying she was amazed by the looks of the little guy, something everyone said when they first saw Reed, who with his long white coat looked more like a rabbit than a cat, especially since he was shy and huddled away from people with his head tucked into his body, shaking. I loved him with everything I had.

"Oh my god, look at him," Jill said. "Look at that cat. I've never seen anything like him."

"Shhhhh," I said. "He's just scared."

We took him back to my apartment and I set him up with his litter box, his food and water. Why hadn't I just told Dad to keep the cat? He needed a companion more than me. In fact, a year later my younger brother Jason went out and bought my father his own cat, but it didn't work out because the animal wouldn't let anyone touch him and spent most of his time hidden in the rafters of the basement, meowing, making my father feel as if he were living inside an Edgar Allan Poe story. Eventually, my dad chose to get rid of that cat too—he was scratching up everything, crying at all hours before disappearing for days only to reappear without warning to start the whole sad cycle again.

The day we brought Reed home was the day Jill finally went out back and spoke to the hippie couple for the first time. Maybe she felt the first scratchings of our family with the addition of the cat. Maybe not. I heard her introduce herself, and they began chatting and laughing about the garden and the weather. Jill's parents were professors, polite people, educated people—she knew her way around small talk. When I looked out my bedroom window, she was holding their baby and smiling like someone in a commercial. The guy too had a frozen look on his face, but he wasn't smiling, and his cheeks were lined with acne scars. His work shirt had a little sewed-on nametag I couldn't read. The tag was white with blue stitching. A few of the people in our program wore similar shirts—ironically. One of the guys who did so had actually hung out with Bob Dylan's son when they were both kids at a private school in New York City. This guy had even been at Dylan's house, for a sleepover, and had once crept down in the middle of the night to take a piss only to see the great bard slumped in front of the blue glow of the television, eating Ring Dings from the box.

The normal thing to do that day would have been to go out and join Jill and the young couple, say something nice about their baby, maybe tell them about the bear I'd seen, but I stayed right where I was, watching them through the curtains. How can I explain this, how I felt almost feral there in the Rattlesnake Creek Apartments? Not just that day, but for the year or two I lived there. I sensed it was a question of biding time, letting it pass. Eventually, the man must have felt himself being watched and turned away from his wife and Jill to look in my direction. I let the curtain drop back into place.

When Jill came back inside, she still had that weird smile going and said they were "nice."

"Nice?" I scoffed.

"What's wrong with you? They were nice."

"I just hate that word."

"That's just silly."

"It's just so fucking fatuous."

"Fatuous? Seriously? What would be better if I said they were fascists, murderers, thieves."

"Yeah, all those are better. At least they sound better."

She looked at me, said nothing, so I went on, "It just doesn't mean anything, right? It's just stupid, and boring, and ordinary."

She laughed, "Are you still talking about the word?"

I shrugged and went into our kitchen and opened the refrigerator.

She followed me, stood behind me, put her hand at the bottom of my skull, and rubbed me there.

"It means they're good," she said. "It means they treat each other well. Why do you have to act like this?"

"Like what?"

The cat cried from the other room. It was maybe about time for beer.

LATER THAT NIGHT, DRUNK, the cat crying in the next room, I told Jill how when I first drove into Missoula I'd taken the Orange Street exit and ended up in the parking lot of St. Pat's Hospital with the rental car still running, a map spread across the steering wheel as I tried to locate myself, and as I sat there peering down at the map, I sort of just shit my pants. Just a wee bit, but it was enough. I'd been on the road too long, I guess. I chuckled, horrified, but didn't move, just stared at the map until I figured out my hotel was just up the road from the hospital, right on the river. The Sweet Rest Motel was the name of the place, a reservation I made from my father's living room while he sat watching *Jeopardy* in the chair my mother had died in when I was a teenager. I lived in that hotel for twenty-seven days before finding the apartment in the Rattlesnake.

Reed finally stopped whining and fell asleep, while Jill

and I made love on the futon in my living room before we too drifted off toward our dreams. Early the next morning, the dark still out, my eyes popped open and I lay there like that for five, maybe six seconds, thinking I was still in South Philly in the apartment above the tax shop, a place where I could smell fried onions and steak wafting into my living room from Geno's Steaks down the block. After the bars closed, the drunks would line up there to get a cheesesteak, voted Best of Philly by the City Paper. The pickup started grinding then, placing me in Montana on the futon with Jill, the grinds like short chortled screams, people trying to get out, and as I looked over at Jill sleeping with her mouth parted and snoring ever so lightly, I thought, open your eyes, open your eyes, open your eyes.

MISSOULA

By THE RIVER WITH Eric's girlfriend, Cassie, I tried to make it better. The gurgle of the Blackfoot was a song beneath the slow, steady chug of my beat-to-shit Audi and the occasional roar of a passing semi. Last night in Missoula, on the way home from the bar, after I'd heard my niece Lucy had been born, I'd kissed Cassie on the lips. It seemed simple enough—I was drunk and happy and horny, but Cassie's boyfriend, a Harvard man, had caught scent of it and gone ape shit, driving up to my place in the Rattlesnake to bang on my door at 3:00 a.m. I was too drunk to be bothered, though, and had slept through the entire episode, so Eric had driven back to his place, feeling crazier now, and, apparently, had thrown Cassie around. Later that morning she was at my door, 7:00 a.m., arm in a sling, a sorry-looking fawn of a girl, telling me the story. The sun was just over the mountain; my mouth soot. I didn't know what she'd wanted, what I could possibly offer, so I asked if she wanted to take a drive. It's what I did in Montana when it was too early to drink and I didn't know what else to do—I'd get in a car and drive. We ended up cruising along the Blackfoot, the water a murky blue in the morning light. It had felt almost right, until it didn't.

"Don't mind me," I said, slowing down. "I'm just going to pull over and puke."

I stumbled from the car to the riverbank, gagging, and I heard her laughing from the car in this pitiful way that even today breaks my heart—all these people trailing around their little balls of hurt and regret. I knew we weren't meant for each other, that we were involved in a stupid yellow affair, but we were only in the middle of it, and I'd have to see it through to whatever end waited. In the least, I had to drive back to Missoula and drop her off at her place, count on Eric not being around.

We hung around the riverbank for a few minutes, skipping stones. I'm sure this was something my father had taught me, though I had no memory of any actual lesson. My father was an old man and his death had hung over me like a guillotine for the last few years, and I might have mentioned something along those lines to Cassie, how much I feared his demise, how angry it made me—people dying, leaving. Why try? Why give a fuck? I don't think she responded to my indulgence. Just a few words from the river, the rushing water over rocks, the birds, the holy green silence of pine trees. I thought of my niece, how her birth countered my fear and trembling, the endless waves of alcohol and talk. The kiss only that: an antidote. Nothing more. How could people fail to understand something so simple? How could I explain it in a way that didn't make me sound like a selfish asshole? Was I a selfish asshole? I tried to quiet my mind, listen to the river.

"Why are you even in Montana?" Cassie finally asked.

"That movie," I'd said.

"Yeah," she said. "A stupid fucking movie."

So many of us were there because of it. Beautiful Brad Pitt slipping his bait under his hat as he wrestled against the current, one hand gripping his fly rod as the water rushed around his hips like a lover's hands. Back in the car, Cassie wiped the spit from my chin, a gesture that made me want her all over again, and we drove back to her place and she asked me up. I went up, and we sat in her apartment, on her sofa, something shimmering between us now, a cat's eyes, a copper nail, moonlight. We watched her snake, a fat python named Gretel she kept in a glass cage where the TV should have been. Over the winter, Gretel had escaped and was on the loose in the apartment complex for a few weeks until Cassie woke up one morning and found the reptile curled up in the corner of its cage. I asked Cassie if I could kiss her again. She said no, but told me I could touch her throat if I'd like. She wanted my hands there.

I did what she wanted, held her like that, just the slightest pressure of my hands on her warm neck.

She said, "I could jerk you off with my good arm."

"OK," I said.

"You have to take it out for me."

I took it out with one hand, my other hand still around her throat. I felt ridiculous now, like I was posing for a still life, but I was willing to let this play out, and in a way this morning wasn't much different than what normally happened to me.

She started jerking me off, and for about a minute it was so close to good, as if this morning might become special, but as if on cue Eric came along and tapped on her window—differently, I'm sure, than his pounding on my door earlier that morning, this a gentle signal between lovers. I could hear the apology in the tap, the effort at reconciliation in the way he whispered her name through the blinds, "Cassie, Cassie." She took her hand off my dick and I released her throat. We were done with each other quicker than a flip of a coin, a line of poetry, daybreak.

She whispered that I must leave, to be very quiet, but I was already up, buckling my black jeans as silent as a ninja. I scampered out the back door of the apartment complex as Eric came in the front. Outside, I slipped down an alley and ducked beneath Cassie's window, the same window where

Eric had just stood, stopping for a moment to listen as they kissed and whispered, my dick still hard. I was spying on my own life.

"Baby, I'm so sorry. I don't know what came over me," Eric cooed.

"It's fine. It's OK, sweetie. I know. I know."

"I won't ever do something like that again."

"Shhh, stop talking now, please, stop talking. It's OK."

I started touching myself through my jeans, but it felt silly, so I stopped and walked across the street, passing the halfway house where old men sat on the porch in lawn chairs and rockers, smoking, playing cards, and telling lies. What time was it? The line of men on the porch reminded me of that Carver story, "Chef's House," and I remembered then or I remember now that Carver, who'd spent some time in Missoula before he became Carver, had based his story on this very place. Or maybe that's wrong. Maybe I'm misremembering some of this. I kept walking as Missoula woke up, low gray clouds over Jumbo. I walked away from my car, not wanting to get back into it, not wanting to go home. I followed Broadway to the bridge, passing the Wilma, crossing over the Clark Fork, the river running low, my mouth a desert, the Great Basin, and my head felt like a cage full of rocks, but it would be a few more years of this before I quit drinking, a few more shipwrecked friendships, and on that morning, I still hadn't had my coffee, so I whispered, "Coffee," as if coffee were my god, and headed to Bernice's, where I could see a few people were spread along the outdoor benches enjoying their coffee in the weak morning light.

A WEEK LATER, I rode out again to the Blackfoot with Cassie after we somehow found ourselves drinking together for a few hours at the Lolo Bar. I intended to set things right. It felt like the honorable thing to do, and at the river I told her how the Blackfeet tribe would give a young warrior a silly name until he killed an enemy. Only then would he get a real name.

"So you're like, what, Throws Up by the River?" she said, laughing.

"Something like that," I said, thinking I just might be able to love her.

But I stuck with the plan, told her I was an asshole, told her I was sorry, told her I couldn't be with her, thinking of that code between guys somehow overlooking the fact that I'd already broken that code with the kiss the night my niece was born, as well as the fact that she had no real interest in being with me.

Despite this, or maybe because of it, she got mad, very mad, and blurted out that she'd been at a party in Lolo the previous weekend and had seen Jill, my ex, and another guy named Eric, a bigheaded guy who favored fashionable bib overalls and now teaches English in China, cuddling in a hot tub. "They were all over each other," she said. Jill and I had been finished for a good two months by then, but the news still fluttered up my ribcage into my throat. Cassie kept twisting the knife. "The whole department was there," she said. My breathing slowed and that underwater feeling sloshed over me. I was surprised how much this bothered me.

"Now maybe you can go get a real name," Cassie said.

"You're kind of an asshole aren't you?" I said.

"Yeah, maybe," she said. "Maybe that means we could have been good together."

"But you don't even like me."

"Stewart, that has absolutely nothing to do with it."

I dropped her off at her apartment, not daring to get out of the car this time, and drove up to Jill's place in the South Hills, where the writer of detective fiction, Jim Crumley, still lived with his third wife and where Jill lived in a basement apartment in a house owned by two lesbian physicians. The couple had a giant shepherd, Iris, a dog that'd been badly abused as a pup before the women had swooped in and saved the poor beast. Jill told me they'd trained the shepherd to attack anyone that entered the yard, especially males. I didn't know if this were a joke, but I'd seen the dog and it looked like a wolf, but bigger, and certainly ready to attack.

That night, I stopped at the fence, considering the sky, the knee-bone moon, my soul. I knew at that moment I was alive to do this. This very thing. Now. Here. I could be ripped apart, but if I went home and sobered up I'd lose courage to confront Jill over her hot tub shenanigans with the other Eric. It would be over between us forever. I knew this to be true somehow, somewhere beneath the reach of language, and wonder now if this were courage, something like nobility, or simple jealousy moving through me, but all that really matters is that I acted—I held my breath and climbed the chain-link fence, scampering across the lawn like a toddler wearing a diaper full of shit, expecting at any moment the dog's paws on my back, his heavy breath, his jaws digging into my neck. Dust to dust. I reached Jill's sliding door and banged on it. No one answered. Banged again. I listened for the dog, but knew he'd already be on me if he were around, so I banged harder, relieved and emboldened. Finally, Jill let me in. She was wearing her pink fluffy robe and eating Cherry Garcia straight from the container. Her hair was damp from the shower and she smelled like peaches. On the TV, *Friends*. I think that was the night she told me David Schwimmer had been in one of her acting classes at Northwestern, right before she explained the business with the other Eric in the hot tub.

"That was nothing," she said, getting a beer. "We were both drunk. You know how I like hot tubs."

Her place was just one giant room with her bed pushed into the corner, her desk next to it, a stack of poetry books there. I saw Mark Strand, Bob Wrigley, Sylvia Plath.

"Yeah," I said, as she went on to tell me about the party, a Missoula house party, how at the end of it a bunch of them drove downtown to the Ox for brains and eggs and then a few of the diehards kept at it, driving to Jerry Johnson to hike into woods, the hot springs there.

"More hot springs? What the hell. How many soaks can you take," I said, wandering over to her bed.

"I can soak for hours—it's spiritual."

"Bullshit. It just feels good."

She shrugged, as if to say what's the difference, but I saw she had something more to tell me.

"What?" I asked, sitting down on her plush green comforter—the one her parents bought her from LL Bean. It was filled with goose-feathers, but had a hole in it that Jill hadn't gotten around to stitching. Sometimes after we'd screwed, I'd pluck the goose feathers from her hair and she'd tell me jokes her father had told her when she was a kid.

"Well, I did meet this Native American guy," Jill said. "It was at Al and Vic's last weekend. He spent the night a couple of times, but I didn't sleep with him. You might have seen him around. He's always in Al's, and he wears this long black trench coat. He has braids."

"OK," I said.

"But I don't really like him. Not really."

"OK."

"But there are some things I like about him."

"Like what?"

She wouldn't tell me, just smiled and said, "He's just really into me, but we didn't sleep together."

OK.

I got her point, saw his braids dipping below her white belly, her breath coming in bubbly gasps, and I pulled her down onto the bed, opened her robe, and got down there with this other guy until she began moaning and grabbing at the sheets, until she closed her eyes, until her neck flushed, until I made her see God.

PIER 59

V IK CALLED THAT DAY in Seattle, my friend Bob Vik.
I was busy in front of the mirror when the phone rang,
busy noticing how my hair was thinning, a crushing blow
for a guy like me—vain, and with a head formerly full of
hair so thick and inviting that random girls, drunk girls,
pretty girls, rude girls, smart girls, many different girls
had approached me simply to ask if they could touch it. I
always said yes, of course, but that was years ago, and now
in Seattle, I was busy running from Jill (who I'd left behind
in Missoula) when Vik called, busy working for the Seattle
Housing Authority, busy and lonely as I stood before my
mirror with my head bent like a penitent, my eyes skyward,
trying to catch a flash of scalp shining through my soon-
to-be-gone locks.

"You want some company in your life, Stewart?" Vik
asked.

Now, you know Bob, Bob Vik, everyone knows Vik.
He's a poet, but he'll be governor one day, for sure—the
only real question is which state. He hails from Kansas, but
ended up in New Orleans via Seattle and before that was
in Missoula for a few years, where I first ran into him. I've
heard post-Katrina that he fled New Orleans for Mon-
terey before heading back to Seattle, but just last week,
bored, I googled Vik and discovered he'd accepted a teaching gig at Santa Cruz. Good for him—Vik, enlightener
of our youth, speaker of truth to the powerless, weaver of
dreams—Bob Vik.

"You know Wrigley's in town," Vik said that afternoon,

his flat Midwestern cadence as slow and sure of itself as a cow chewing cud. He went on: "And I've got women. Dos."

Wrigley was a famous, i.e. published, poet that we both knew from our grad school days in Missoula. He was in Seattle as a part of a literary panel at the annual Seattle Book Fest, and though the thought of a room full of literary types in an echoey warehouse along the waterfront left me nauseous with dread, I agreed at once.

"Yeah, that sounds cool," I said, tasting the loneliness of each syllable.

"Sounds cool? Listen to you, Simmons. You're hilarious."

WE ALL DROVE IN Bob's beater Cadillac to Pier 59 and parked it under the I-5 overpass, semis roaring overhead, the girls as shiny and beautiful as sunlight on water as we walked to the pier. Bob's date, Ronnie, was an architect working on the new football stadium along the edges of downtown. My date, Eileen, shared my birthday, Feb. 19, and strangely enough, I'd already met her earlier that year at the 30th birthday party I threw for myself at the Rattlesnake Creek Apartments in Missoula before I fled Jill and that town. And though it was only November of that very year, that party seemed like years ago, and when I asked Eileen about it in Seattle she remembered nothing of it. Understandable considering she'd showed up with Vik, drunk, leaning into him, never breathing a word about the fact that it was her birthday too. She was a worse drunk than me, I guessed, but a nice one, and young enough that the drink hadn't yet touched her looks. She was skinny, but curvy in the right places with a face as sweet as candy. When I looked at her I tried not to think about Jill back in Missoula working for the YWCA at her sad little secretarial job.

In the warehouse, tables were stacked with obscure books and earnest panelist, and we wandered around until we found Wrigley, chatting him up some before we bolted for a bar to begin the elaborate ritual of getting into the pants of these lovely young women. Our first stop was a beer joint in Ballard, a working-class neighborhood where the wet air felt stewy and smelled of fish from the locks down the block, a place where it was possible to view salmon fighting for home so they could spawn in familiar waters before dying.

In Seattle not all the bars served liquor, only the lucky ones. Many establishments were just beer joints, such as our place in Ballard, but the place next door served the hard stuff, and when the part of the evening requiring shots arrived, Bob came up with a plan. Us boys would run next store, down a shot, order another one and bring those back in our mouths for the girls. The girls agreed at once and when we returned with the shots they opened their mouths like hatchlings as we feed them their smoky bourbon.

And it was about this time, right after we'd fed them their shots, that Bob had excused himself to the head for a piss, and Bob's girl had said a funny thing. I'd turned to her, this lovely, willowy architect and, thinking myself suave, said, "You know, a friend of mine once said, 'Poets are pussies.'" I thought this line would at least shock her, but she simply rolled her eyes and shot back, "No, poets *get* pussy."

I couldn't help but smile, showing my bad teeth. This was the direction of our evening, and my life back then— wherever drink took me I went, letting whatever spill from my mouth. When Bob settled himself back at the table, I brought up my inevitable bald spot, and the big man looked stricken. He laughed me off, saying, "Stewart, the only hairs that count are on the sides—you know that."

This made perfect sense at the time, and still does, but what I haven't told you about Bob was that twice he'd try to humiliate me, once, by convincing me a bicycle pump could get me high (technically, a fact), and once, when we had a quick moral argument in a bar in Missoula in the middle of another ill-planned evening together. I'd said something about the emptiness of life, the lack of any universal morality, and how at any given moment anyone could do just about anything. It was the type of talk in which only the young partake, especially a certain type of earnest male who likes to drink.

"But that's the point," he said. "People don't. They don't do just anything."

"But they could. I mean I could just murder someone, anyone—randomly. That doesn't scare you? That doesn't make it all meaningless?"

"But you won't," he said, and he was right, and it's why, despite his girth, Bob always got the women. He was usually right. He was smarter than everyone else, and funnier too.

But the day in the bar with those women wasn't about anything but the fact that from the start, because of our shared birthdays, this woman and I understood we would share our bodies, eventually. The only curiosity was how we were going to get there, and whether it was going to be that night or another, which reminded me of how it was with the men back in Philly. And maybe thinking of such, it was right then, right after Bob said the thing about the hair on both sides of one's head, when I took Eileen's hand and guided it under the table and placed it atop my cock. She accepted it, stroking me through my jeans for a glorious five or ten minutes as Bob and his woman kept up their ironic banter. It was one of the few times I felt I'd outsmarted Bob, and I wanted so much to tell him and the architect what my girl was doing beneath the table, but I just smiled and sipped my drink, letting it all happen. For once, I knew enough to keep my mouth shut. The truth is I don't even remember this girl's name (though I call her Eileen here), but I loved her almost as much as any of the others because she gave me this moment, the crowning glory of my youth—something straight from a movie, but better.

And as she stroked me, and as Bob and his woman quieted down, we began to speak about Feb 19, a cusp day, and my girl told me she'd always identified as an Aquarius, while I saw myself as more of a Pisces. "Maybe that's a metaphor," I said. And maybe that's why later that night it all went to shit when I bit her while still inside her, just a gentle nibble on her shoulder, really, but enough to make her cry, and just enough to break my riddled heart. I realize now it wasn't the bite, it was what the bite signified. It was the fact that we were alone together in her bed and meant so little to each other, while in the bar at least we had the elicit thrill of her stroking me through my jeans in a roomful of people. So she cried while I was inside her, and I stopped and thought of Rita, how Rita had never cried while we fucked, even that first time when I'm sure it hurt and she did her best to pretend otherwise. I got out of bed then, put on my clothes, and left.

She called once more, this girl, and we talked about meeting up, but never did. Instead, Jill visited a week later, deciding to stay and study yoga, before we eventually moved back to Montana. Jill and I spent our last night in Seattle sucking down clams on the pier, not too far from the warehouse where Bob and I had taken the girls to meet Wrigley, and I realized I was making a gigantic mistake by returning to Montana, but by then it was too late.

But I need to say one more thing about Vik, about that night.

When we dropped Bob and his girl off at his place, as he got out of the car (and this was the first time I realized it wasn't his car we were driving, but my girl's car), he'd looked me in the eye and said as seriously as I'd ever heard him say anything, "Darcie doesn't know anything about this, Stewart," and I smiled, remembered the air pump, and said, "Sure, Bob, that sounds good," again tasting the loneliness of each syllable. Later, in New Orleans, where I had my last drink (what better place!), and when all of the old gang were back together in a bar the night before Bob was to marry Darcie, we were deciding on which bar to hit next when Bob looked me in the eye and something of that night in Seattle, mixed ever so slightly with that moral argument we had way back in Missoula, passed between us.

"I don't think so," Vik said in New Orleans. "I'm done. I'm good. I'll see you guys tomorrow."

Yes, I could do anything, I'd told him in Missoula, and surely he knew I might just get drunk enough in New Orleans that I'd spill the beans to Darcie about those girls in Seattle.

Now, in Nebraska, sitting here watching a game, I hear the man on TV say something about a stadium in Seattle, how it funnels all the noise directly down onto the field making it an exceedingly difficult place for a visiting squad to play, and in the next moment, I realize it's the stadium Bob's architect-friend was working on because she'd said something about the acoustics of the place too, said it just a few moments before I'd made my ridiculous comment about poets and pussies. In fact, it was one of the reasons

I'd said what I said—I had nothing to say about the acoustics of a football stadium (and still don't!), so once again, slumped in my chair watching a game, those women come back to me as shiny and beautiful as sunlight on water, and I lean closer, trying to hear, to see, to understand that boy who fathered the man.

SOFT CITY SEATTLE

JILL CAME TO SEATTLE—Jill, a jokey brunette with a wide
Carly Simon mouth, a girl I was sure I could love. I worked
as a temp for the SHA, the Seattle Housing Authority,
filing forms in triplicate, sneaking into the bathroom for a
post-lunch jerk every now and then. It wasn't a bad place to
work, just sad, filled with lines of low-income folks looking
for affordable housing, trying to figure a way around the
surreally stupid catch-22 placement criteria of having the
same address for at least a year before you were placed in a
new home. Hardly anyone seeking assistance had lived in
the same place for a year. That was the point. That was why
they were there. That was why they had risen early, skipped
work, taken two buses, a plastic number, Styrofoam cups
of coffee and waited for three hours in the cramped lobby
with its fluorescent lighting and mean little rows of metal
folding chairs. At least once a day, one of the home seekers,
who were mostly poor and black, cracked once they got
word of the bureaucratic bit of nonsense sitting between
them and a decent place to live. They'd start hooting and
hollering, what-the-fucking their way out the front door.
I loved that point in the day. It felt like a coffee break,
the screamer upsetting every ounce of dumb office deco-
rum, screaming at the sad-sack placement clerks, who were
mostly old, sandal-and-sock wearing hippies looking for
an easy-going gig. This wasn't it. My own drifting ways had
moved me twenty times in ten years, three different states
so I was always touched by the home seekers' anger. Me,
a guy with two degrees, filing forms that left my thumbs

chalky with black, probably cancer-causing carbon dust. This was 1996. My heart was on fire.

One day, my friend Sean showed up on a Saturday wearing his smile.

We were headed out for some Taco Bell but first he showed me the gun. Since I'd last seen him, about six months ago, right before I left Montana, Sean had grown his hair long and that day in Seattle he was wearing it in a ponytail, which he kept fiddling with, putting his arms behind his head to fool with the rubber band, debanding his tail before banding it up again and again. The long hair, but more the behind-the-head gesture when he was fooling with his hair, gave him a vague Christ-like look. It was one of those rubbery moments when he took the gun, a little .22, from his duffel bag and gave it to me like a whisper to a stranger. He was in town for only a few hours, between flights. He was heading to California, I think. Sean was from Alabama, though he grew up in Houston so he didn't have much of a drawl. He had shiny, intelligent eyes, and a friendly band of freckles that stretched across his forehead and leaked down onto his cheeks like tears. Taking the gun, I cupped my hands, stupidly, like I was twelve and catching water for a drink from the spigot in my driveway after a hot night of release tag with my friends. We'd always stay out late, long after the street lamps came on and the fireflies emerged. We'd bat the bugs out of the air with whiffle ball bats, their tiny insect bodies making a satisfying popping sound when the bats made contact.

That day with Sean was the second time I'd touched a gun. The first was with my crazy friend Barry in the Bitterroot when we lined our Coors empties on a flat rock atop a mountain. Barry took a .44 Magnum from his glove compartment, and we paced our paces before shooting. The gun had a barrel that looked twice as long as my dick, and as I squeezed its trigger each booming shot jolted up my arms into my shoulders before echoing back at us from the valley below. Boom-boom. Boom-boom. In the distance, beneath that, we heard dogs howling.

"It's not loaded," Sean said that day in my apartment, snatching the gun out of my cupped hands, a little disgusted. "And the safety is on anyway."

"That's cool," I said, hoping Jill, who was at yoga, didn't pop back in before we stepped out for lunch.

Jill had discovered yoga in Seattle, and six times a week walked down the block to the studio where the windows were painted white. Last week, she'd run in flush-faced, excited, showing me a new move, posture, position, whatever you call those contortions, the breathing. It spooked me the way she squatted on the floor, put her palms flat between her thighs and leaned forward, rising up and balancing all her precious weight on her tender white palms. Her body was learning a new language in those days, and I'd hear it and almost gulp, knowing there was a good chance I might not be able to keep up—or want to. They all had names, these poses, and the one she did that day made her look like a crane and she called it The Crane.

For some reason Sean and I didn't realize our friendship was basically over. Before I'd moved away from Missoula to Seattle, we'd gotten drunk at a bar in Lolo and rode home in the back of someone's pickup, the cold air biting at our ears and fingertips as we lay flat in the pickup, staring up at the western sky until it felt like we weren't moving at all. The bad cold and good sky a pair of dice, pain and beauty shaken together in a cup. By the time we got home in the pickup, my fingers were numb and I challenged Sean to a fight. When we unloaded ourselves from the truck we jitter-boxed down an alley, half-fooling and totally serious, where dumpsters loaded with rotten fruit gave off a gassy, medicinal odor, like ether. We started calling each other names until I shoved my chin close to his and dared him to punch me in the face, which he did three times, blackening one eye. I told stories about my black eye all weekend. People bought me drinks, calling Sean a son-of-a-bitch. One thing is I can't entirely remember why Sean had a gun that day in Seattle, but it had something to do with his girlfriend's niece, whose mother's live-in boyfriend was molesting. Sean said if asked, he would shoot this man, and I remember shaking my head and saying, "yes," though I'm not entirely sure I did.

"Where's Jill?" he asked as he put the gun way and we gathered our things to go to Taco Bell.

"She's at yoga."

"Oh yeah, I didn't know she was into that."

"She's into it since we moved here."

He nodded sagely, didn't make a joke about new sexual positions or the such, but his forehead did turn redder as if he had. Sean was always a little vague when it came to Jill and it would be years before I understood. Apparently, he had made a pass at Jill, maybe more, when we all first met at graduate school in Montana. Jill told me this a few years after we left Seattle, while in New Orleans, during the weekend wedding of another of our grad-school friends, Bob Vik, as we sat on the porch of our B&B in the Garden District on a street shaded by magnolias, making me promise, before she told me, that I wouldn't get mad. I got mad.

I came home from that wedding, my insides bruised, my liver aching, and instead of watching Bush beat Gore with a sixer and some wine, I stayed up long into the night, until the very bitter end, which turned out only to be a beginning, when Gore's limousine turned around midway to his concession speech. If I had been drinking I would have been asleep for hours by then, but instead, there I was, watching it live, listening to Wolf Blitzer. This seemed momentous at the time, that I was sober, late at night, watching TV, and witnessing something important happening, something I might even tell my children about. I couldn't believe Sean would do that. The pass, I mean. But it's the truth. It's what happened.

On the porch in New Orleans, as we sipped drinks from our sweaty pitcher of gin and tonics, Jill began to tell me by asking a question, "Remember that time I left the party, my party, the Christmas party at my house? The time when Daniel got really drunk during Truth or Dare?"

I remembered. Jill had disappeared in the middle of the festivities, just about the time Daniel, some trust-fund asshole from New York, was removing his pants on a dare. It was cold outside. I sat in the kitchen as Mr. Trust Fund (who would later go on to publish notable fiction in *The New Yorker*) removed his briefs to the hoots of the growing crowd in the living room. During the commotion, Sean, the ever-valiant knight, the misplaced Southern Gentleman, slipped down the back stairs to look for Jill, whom he found dreaming under a pine tree. Later that night, after we made love, I picked the pine needles from her hair and asked her why she had drifted away from the party like that. I don't remember her answer, but apparently, Sean had kissed her when he had found her. I imagined them rolling out from under the tree to sit with their shoulders touching, watching the yellow stars dappled densely across the heavens. The sky in Montana was always, at least, part of the story, like the first night I met Sean. We were driving back from a professor's party at a ranch in Stevensville, where during the ride there, I'd seen not only my first real live buffalo, a creature I thought extinct, but a llama too. Halfway home Sean had pulled over at a Conoco station, springing out of his truck to scramble up the side of a hill as I followed, brambles ripping at our hands as we spread the prickly branches and moved to the top where the sky was so beautiful we grew bored looking at it after only a few seconds. Something so perfect, could teach us nothing, we knew. We compared the cuts on our hands and forearms, instead.

"Did you kiss him back," I said, that sweltering afternoon in New Orleans, feeling excited, crazy and dead all at once. Dully, I knew how important this was. I tried to pay attention to my life, but we were almost out of gin.

"No I didn't kiss him back. I stopped him."

"How did you stop him?"

"I just stopped him. I told him I was into you."

"But we weren't even a couple yet. I mean, not really."

"I liked you right away, you know that."

"But you wouldn't tell me right away. Or now. I mean if you hooked up with him. You wouldn't tell me."

"I'm telling you now. I didn't hook up with him. He kissed me once and then I told him to stop."

THE FUNNY THING IS at the end of all this Jill and I get kids. We're still together, but if you had told me that then, that day, sitting stiffly on my plastic green couch with Sean showing me his gun, I would have chuckled and then looked steady-dead into your eyes and said a little too seriously, "No, man, you miss my point. That's not what I'm trying to say here," like when I told my sister I was marrying Jill, and she said, "Really, I always thought you guys were more like buddies."

•

A COUPLE OF SEVEN-LAYER burritos later, Sean and I went down the hall to Mr. Amens' place, a small, Chinese-looking older dude whom I liked to visit. He was always alone, except for his dog, Chance, and he was always home, always wearing baggy black wool pants, an oxford shirt, usually shoeless. Bald, he had a little soul patch. All day long, I guessed, he shuffled around alone his apartment, which had the exact, L-shaped layout as our place, except his was filled with stacks of newspapers, magazines, and shoe boxes which lined the walls of his place and spilled from the closets. Amens was almost crazy, it seemed, but he was also something of a saint, in my eyes, though my Catholic days were long gone. Amens told me how he once put an ad in the paper, pretending to be blind, requesting a reader, and keeping at it a few times before calling the whole thing off.

"To be honest, I felt like a pervert," he explained, "Sitting there listening to this girl pretending not to see her, sneaking peeks as she read."

I had so many questions; I didn't know where to begin.

"Was she pretty?" I asked. "Did she ever do anything weird when she read to you?"

"Weird? Like what, pick her nose?"

"Weirder."

"Weirder. Listen to you. You got one of those bad imaginations. Isn't it enough to say I felt dirty doing what I did so I stopped?"

"No, that's definitely not enough," I said, taking a pull off my beer. I usually brought a six-pack when I visited Amens. "You're the one that put the ad in. Why did you say you were blind? Why tell me the story if you're not going to tell the story?"

"I'm telling you. I don't know. It was something to do. It was an experiment."

"Did you pull it off? Did she ever suspect you could see?"

He became uncomfortable talking about it, so he showed me instead, acting blind like that. He sat stiffly in his red chair with his hands on his knees, occasionally scratching his palm with the fingers of his other hand. I rose up and paced in front of him as we talked, doing little tricks like pretending to drop my beer or shaking my head back-and-forth, but he kept it up pretty well, never blinking out of place or moving his eyes in my direction even when I crouched down close enough to his face to see the specks of green in his irises and smell the onions on his breath. He just stared ahead like I wasn't even there.

Later, I found out Amens couldn't read at all and that was why he had pretended to be blind. Like a lot of us, he was too embarrassed to tell the truth. All he wanted was someone to read to him, stories, or made-up things as he called them. I was amazed when he told me this, not believing it. We were stoned, looser than usually, and he put on some screeching, low-country delta blues and I asked how he could do his art without reading. Yes, Amens was an artist. Practically everyone I knew in those days was an artist of some kind, except maybe my sister. Amens' art was the found kind—he collected things with a capital T, mostly random scraps of papers: matchbooks, ticket stubs, receipts, old menus, a list of words from an eighth-grade spelling test. "Consciousness" one of the words, I remember. He put it all together like a puzzle, cutting up the paper, and lining the pieces on corkboard so they told a funny little story that was always nonsensical with some truth sprinkled on, like kids' glitter, which he sometimes used. When I asked how he did this without reading, he

·

THE THING IS AMENS died. Not then but later, after I moved back to Montana with Jill to take a job as a high school sportswriter. Jill had spotted the advertisement at the library where she'd read the out-of-town papers. After studying with Mir for about a year, she wanted to move back to Montana and open her own studio, which she eventually did. Her place had blond-oak floors and a sauna in the back, next to the windowless room where they practiced the hot yoga. She sold soups and salads, some sandwiches. On the lobby wall was a mural of two women with their hands clasped above their heads so their conjoined bodies were in the shape of a mountain. At the end of each session, she went around to her students and placed the felt bags on their foreheads. I ended up interviewing high school football coaches. Wrestlers. Boys who dieted religiously and groped in unitards, telling me afterwards, "You have to want it." Cross country runners were some of the smartest people I knew. They talked about endurance, pacing yourself, how you could imagine an entire race, step-by-step, the night before the race. It's over before the gun goes off, they said—the run like an afterthought. A lot of their language made sense to me, not like the football coaches and their war metaphors, their talk of carnage, but I liked the basketball guys the most, especially the coaches who emphasized a running game over defense, how they preached speed and precision. Something like that was beautiful to watch. I realized most of what these coaches said would stick with their athletes more than anything a teacher might tell them.

When Jill and I left Seattle, I left behind the ungodly green plastic couch I purchased from a catalog, the one Sean and I sat on that day, and which still is the single most uncomfortable piece of furniture I've ever owned, and that's saying something. I had lugged it all the way from Montana to Seattle, but I left it in the basement of our apartment complex when I returned to Montana to become a sportswriter. Leaving it had felt like a sacrifice, a strange little ritual.

A few years ago, we visited Seattle, Jill and I. We visited the old place and I wanted to see if the couch was still there. It wasn't, and I went upstairs to Amens' place, admitting only then that was why I had returned here, not only to the apartment complex, but to Seattle. I wanted to see my old friend. I went up to the sixth floor, 649. We lived at the other end, 609, the two apartments separated by a stretch of open-air patio. I was thrilled and sick as I knocked on the door, the damp Seattle air like all those times I visited my friend, usually with a sixer in hand. I don't think many people change—not because they can't, but because they won't.

When I knocked on Amens' door, an old woman in a head scarf and glasses answered. I asked about Amens and she shook her head, saying she had lived here twenty years and there was no Amens. And here's the thing, here's the reason I've taped together all these ridiculous memories—there was one glorious moment when I believed her in this way, that she had lived there, not Amens for the last twenty years, and that I had only dreamt about my visits to Amens, dreamt, perhaps my whole time in that soft city, where, you know, of course, it rains all the time and where I went days without ever feeling dry, when for one reason or another I wore the same slightly soggy undergarments for several days and caught a bad cold. My mind raced. Maybe I was on the wrong floor—but there was no way I could make that mistake. Jill and I used to joke about 609. No, it

was maybe a good five seconds of limbo, as I rocked there
on my heels listening to this old woman groan on, that I
glimpsed into the empty inside of a life, not mine or Jill's,
but a third one, one who has walked with us this entire
time. I wonder if it's still there now, this third one, happily
going about its business. It's a feeling I can still call up, if I
concentrate, if I close my eyes and pretend. It's the feeling
of waking up in a strange bed and for a few sneaky seconds forgetting your life. You feel in touch with something
larger than yourself, what some people call God or irony.
Yes, of course, I had imagined the entire thing. There was
no Amens, but then I heard what the woman was actually
saying to me. I understood her now. She was saying Amens
had died. She was his widow, the sad one, and she had
lived there the entire time. Was I an old friend of his? she
asked. He had a lot of friends. He died a couple years back,
she explained. She came home one day and found him in
his chair, gone, and that was that. Heart failure. I nodded,
telling her I was sorry. She invited me inside, offering mint
tea and ginger snaps. We had an OK talk, but he was all
cleaned out of there, Amens was, and though I thought I
recognized some of the furniture, it was too unsettling so I
didn't linger. At the doorway, before I left, I asked her what
Amens' mother's maiden name was.

"That's such a curious question," she said, "Why would
anyone ask that?"

I shrugged. "I'm a curious guy."

She smiled and shook her head and said, "That's not
good enough."

"OK, I'm curious and maybe I've come with a sack
of money to say, 'Here, take this. I knew him. He meant
something to me. He was a friend of mine.'"

She laughed, showing strong, white teeth, "You poor boy.

I can't believe he never told you about me, but I think I can understand that. He had his own ways. I'm sure he liked you." I smiled back at her.

"Gill," she said, answering my question before closing the door.

When I came back to our hotel room after visiting Amens' widow, Jill waited in the Warrior pose, the furniture rearranged, the TV muted. Between breaths, she asked where I'd been. I didn't tell her, couldn't. We don't talk like that anymore. Instead, I just said I went to Taco Bell, had a seven-layer burrito. She grimaced, breathed deeply through her nostrils, held it for a moment, and then released it slowly, softly through her mouth, before telling me, "Someday, that stuff is going to kill you."

JAMAICA WEDDING

I WAS IN JAMAICA with my friend Ted, the serial killer, who was hitching up with his first wife, a local woman he'd met at LaSalle University in Philadelphia, where they'd studied psychology and coauthored a master's thesis entitled *The Diorama of the Diseased Mind*. The day they hooked up, I was with him and the rest of my cronies lubricating myself for a reading at a used bookstore in Center City. I'd won a writing contest, and some literary types were kind enough to publish a chapbook of a story of mine called *Dying to be Released*. The story was about a woman who calls a man to get a bird out of her apartment. The bird, a pigeon, had flown into her high-rise efficiency through an open window and the man had arrived wide-eyed and breathless, ready to be a hero. When he stepped into her apartment, he'd found the bird sitting still in the far corner, eying him. It goes on from there, utter lies. The cronies and I had been drinking since lunch, rolling from one bar to the next along the trash-strewn streets of Philadelphia as we celebrated my admittance into the heady club of published writers. Little did I know that this was it for my literary career, my zenith, this little bird tale—my one night in Paris. I would not publish another story.

I stepped into the bookstore, the door's bell jiggling. Stacks of books spilled off the shelves into piles on the floor, this a few years before the chains swallowed the industry whole. Pointillist art hung blithely from its blue walls. The woman who'd chosen my manuscript from a slush pile rushed to hug me. She smelled of strawberries and secrets, and over her left shoulder, waiting in a tidy clump of folding metal chairs in front of a plywood podium, lurked the audience. My audience, like mourners at a wake. In the crowd, I saw my father and brother, both now gone, watching me with their sad eyes. Drunk, I read, dedicating the story to my uncle, the most freshly dead one, who a month earlier had read the same story on his deathbed and pronounced it "pretty good," which was high praise from the clan of Irish-Catholic lunatics who raised me. What I remember about the story is how it ends with the narrator gathering the hurt bird into his hands, bringing the bird to his chest in a gesture of vulnerability and healing, of hope, a small redemptive moment not without beauty—the very best I had to offer.

At the reception after the reading, on a patio strung with Christmas lights, a stranger approached me with a pen, paper, and a smile. He asked for my autograph, again the one and only time this would happen in my life. This night, a night of firsts and lasts.

Jamaica was after all this, but it was on this night, right after the reading, when my crew headed to yet another bar, when Ted had left us to woo his future Jamaican bride.

"I think she likes me. Can you believe that—me?" Ted had asked at McGlinchey's, gathering his things to leave, the jukebox wailing Patsy Kline, Hank Williams waiting in the wings.

"What's she like?" I asked.

"She's a nice girl," Ted said. "I don't want to fuck her over."

"That's noble," I said.

"And she's from Jamaica," he said, his eyes dancing. "Her father owns a franchise of bakeries."

"The Baker's Daughter. Great. Have another shot." I pushed a double of Jameson toward him—neat, poured to

the very lip of the glass. He eyed it for a second or two, his life ebbing on its burnt-orange surface
"Nah, I'm out of here."

JUST A FEW MONTHS later, I'd stumble off to Montana to earn an MFA, a move that would utterly strip me of my urge to write. After I graduated, after Seattle, I took a job as a sportswriter, and, believe it or not, the job felt like a victory of sorts (at least I was getting paid to write!), so when I received Ted's invitation to his wedding in Jamaica, I quickly decided a trip there would make for a perfect celebration.

And this is what happened.

The wedding was in the books. Two other of Ted's friends, Kit and Jay, along with myself, sat in a club. Kit sat on Jay's lap, facing him, the two of them kissing as if the guy sitting next to them, me, was not actually there, which in a metaphoric sense I wasn't. They hardly knew each other, these two—both had come from New York where they worked together on some Conde Nast fashion magazine, and just last night we'd all skinny-dipped in the Caribbean, forming a tangled little circle in the ocean as we bobbed in the warm water like fetuses. But it wasn't all fun and games. Earlier that same evening, I'd been punched in the jaw by a Jamaican cop while in a Jamaican bathroom stall, where I had gone repeatedly to snort some Jamaican blow we'd just bought in a Jamaican alley. The punch had felt so authentically Jamaican that I was sure I was being filmed—not in the usual sense, when you feel a camera on you, but rather when you *know* the camera is there watching because the moment feels so important, so dangerous, so real. A YouTube moment years before YouTube.

But the punch was done. Now, Kit (who after the cop

had punched me, and I'd emerged from the bathroom wide-eyed and found Jay and her waiting, had reached for my hand and taken it softly in hers. And in that single touch, coming so soon after the punch, I'd felt all the love that is possible in this world, and knew, under the right circumstances, that we could be happy together forever) and Jay were still kissing, and my jaw still ached from the punch as if I had given someone, say, Jay, a blowjob, which is maybe—sleeping with Kit aside, and living happily-ever-after with either her or Jill, way back in Montana, *Montana* for Christ's sake—what I wanted the most.

But I won't talk about that. The story here is I didn't understand my desires, didn't know what questions to ask, nor how to become the person I wanted to become, and with Kit and Jay kissing like that, and no one kissing me, I decided to not actually be there any longer, and went outside and stood under an orange moon, not really believing it could be the same moon shining down on my life back in Montana. Different planet, different moons.

"You look a little lost, man," called over a guy leaning against a cab. "What do you need, marijuana? Woman?"

This was one question I'd been waiting for all my life. It felt like a gift. He was short, dark-skinned, and wore an orange and blue Miami Dolphins T-shirt, along with a bowler hat adorned with a single feather. I trusted his eyes.

"Woman," I said. "Yeah, I need a woman." I looked like a rich man, I guess, because I'd been in the wedding party and had worn a tuxedo with a dark green velvet vest holding in my sportswriter's pudge, which only three months into the job had already started to sprout. (And by the end of that year I would be so plump from beer and gymnasium cheeseburgers, pizza, and dogs, that my father wouldn't recognize me when I returned to Boothwyn, PA for Christmas. And though I eventually lost the weight, returning to my string-bean self, Dad would never leave this fat me behind, gently teasing me about it until the day he died, the bastard.)

That night, though, I jumped into the man's cab and he began jabbering on as we navigated the streets, and again I began to feel that this was the kind of *authentic* experience, raw and real, that I craved. I hadn't been convinced (and I'm still not) that life as language is a construct, that a table is only a table because we have collectively decided to call it a table. Bullshit is bullshit, and I wanted to know a table as a table by banging my head against it until it hurt. Call me a romantic—I think I even told the cabbie something like this, told him I loved him, loved the moment, and when I said all this, he just looked at me, and I can still see his eyes on me in the cab's mirror, still feel them there. It took me years to understand that certain kinds of honesty, in certain kinds of situations, simply aren't desired. It scares people. And in those days, I was always most honest when I was drunk.

The cabbie took me to a lonely dirt road lined with metal shacks and women standing outside of them, the women mostly fat and dark, and the thought of being with any of them terrified me.

"See what you like, man?"

"God, no."

"Really, man? It's more if we go to the club."

"How much more?"

"How much you got? It's $150 at the club."

"Yeah, OK the club."

I half-thought he might take me back to the club holding Kit and Jay, and I prayed that they would be gone and I could find my whore in peace, but he took me somewhere new, another place densely packed with bodies, all of the men white, all the woman dark and pretty in neon-colored polyester cocktail dresses. Many were holding glittery purses and wore strings of fake pearls. My cabbie knew the muscled-up dreadlocked guy at the door wearing a Buffalo Bills—San Francisco 49ers Super Bowl T-shirt. He spoke with an American accent, this guy, and I wondered if he were like me—out here searching for the sheltering sky. They grinned and slapped hands, talking for what seemed liked hours as I stood next to them, swaying in the breeze, thinking that perhaps this wasn't the best of ideas. I'd already been punched once in the face by a Jamaican cop—and I'd seen *Midnight Express* as a boy, but when I looked up at the sky that night all I saw was Jack Kerouac's ruined face sketched there in the stars, telling me to keep moving, keep doing, that we all die eventually.

Finally, then, inside the club, I scored a woman with gigantic breasts, but in the next minute she was gone, and we left instead with a slender woman, a bit older, who slid into the backseat of the cab with me and immediately put her hand on my dick and began rubbing me through my expensive rental pants, the cab driver's eyes flashing on us in the rear-view mirror. We had agreed on an amount, and he drove past more tin shacks as I wondered exactly where we were going. My woman thought I was a rich American. I thought she was a whore, a lovely dark-skinned whore that I would always remember. Not once did we kiss, and more than anything about this night I wish I had the memory of this, the courage of a single kiss.

Eventually we stopped in front a dingy-looking hotel carved from the middle of a grove of palm trees. The Patriot. Really just another shack with a neon sign. It was ridiculous and nowhere, exactly like a place I kept locked inside my heart. The woman still had her hand on my dick. The plan was to go up to the room and do our business, but I knew I would get beaten and robbed, and I felt myself almost wanting this. I think I bought the whole thing because of the neon sign. It had to be a real hotel.

"You ready?" she asked.

I hesitated, caught the driver's gaze. "Don't leave me," I said, pleading with my eyes.

He laughed as if I'd just read a joke from a book.

"Sure, man, go on up there. I'll wait right here."

I went inside. The room was sterile, antiseptic. I could have been in Nebraska. The woman went into the bathroom, ran the water. I took off my clothes and lay stupidly on the bed, thinking myself big and ready. I held my dick in my hand. She stepped out in a negligee, looking lovely and a little lost. She laughed at me, holding my dick like that, and I wondered, drunkenly, how my size compared with the other men from the club, to say nothing of the Jamaican men she had known. The thought of these men stirred me.

"Let's do the money, first," she said and we did and then she fell into bed, first sucking me for a minute or two and then pulling me down on top of her. It was all too mechanical.

"Wait," I said, and we began again, but this time I turned her around and we starting going at it like that, and I just wanting to get it over with really. I didn't really think of Jill. That was the point, I didn't think of anything.

When I was done, she turned her head and said with unmistakable disappointment in her voice, "Damn, I was just getting into it," the words, like a slap to my temple, waking me up.

Outside, the sky had darkened. I expected to see an empty spot where the cab had been, a knock on the back of my head. But there it was, the cab, still waiting, gas drifting out of its exhaust like an old man's pipe. I crawled into the backseat. Maybe this was part of it. Maybe this is where it would happen, but the driver just smiled and asked if I'd kissed her, his eyes in the mirror different than the smile, as furious as my father's.

"No, Jack," I said. "I didn't"

He laughed his sound-track laugh, shaking his head, liking that I called him Jack, I guessed. I shrugged and smiled back, and asked if he'd ever read Jack Kerouac or Paul Bowles.

"Bowles is better," I said.

"No, man," he said. "I don't read. There's too much living to be done."

"Amen to that," I said.

"Amen?"

"Yeah, amen—God, you know. Bless me father. All of that."

"No. God I don't joke with. I don't mess with God."

"Why the hell not, man?" I said, happy that the talk had turned philosophical, but the air in the cab had changed and he pulled the car off the road, shut off the ignition, and turned to me with a look in his eyes I did not recognize.

"Who do you think are, Mr. American?"

"What? What's wrong?" I said.

"What's wrong with you?"

I didn't say anything, and we stared at one another as the sounds of the surrounding shacks filtered in—a stray laugh, the howl of a dog, a baby's cry, the clack of an air conditioner.

"Who the hell are you?" he asked.

"I'm a sports writer. I'm here for my friend's wedding," I said, knowing as the words left my lips that they were not enough, that I would have to give more.

TWIN FALLS

JILL AND I MADE a game of moving away from one another before coming back together, hiding ourselves inside ourselves, afraid to admit something, I guess. I kept drinking for the release of it, the feeling that it could lead somewhere new, somewhere better. One night, drunk, just a few days before I was due to move to Seattle and begin my new life there as a file clerk for the Seattle Housing Authority, I got into it with my best friend Sean. Sean was on the short side, and, in the heat of the moment, I ended up calling him, "a little man, a midget, a very fucking tiny person," but Sean was also from Alabama and tough as a snake, and he ended up punching me in the face a few times as I kept asking for it even as he beat the shit out of me, blackening both of my eyes.

The memory of this fight saddened me until, a few years later, in New Orleans for the wedding of Bob Vik, when I learned Sean had made a move on Jill in Montana.

"He made me swear never to tell you," Jill told me over drinks, the delta heat prickly on our skin, something inside clawing to get out.

"OK," I said.

After leaving Missoula, we stayed in Seattle for almost a year before hightailing it back to Montana, where I covered high school sports as a reporter in the Bitterroot. Jill, sweet girl, found me the job. I did that for another year before taking my act to a bigger paper in Twin Falls, the town where Evel Knievel had jumped the Snake River in his modified rocket-cycle. Twin Falls was populated by Mormons, outdoor freaks, and just plain freaks. They called it the Magic Valley for the way dams and canals off the Snake River had turned this dead stretch of southern Idaho into a fertile oasis. The pulpy sweet smell of sugar beets, soy beans, and wheat hung in the air throughout the summer and early fall. A hundred miles up the road, along the edges of the Sawtooth Forest, Hemingway had put a bullet in his brain at his summer home in Ketchum. My plan was something different, my plan was to work myself up the newspaper food chain. I had dreams, suddenly. I had visions. I saw myself on ESPN, my name stenciled on the screen beneath my face, my whitened teeth glistening.

But I was in Twin Falls for just a few days before the strange listlessness of the place fell over me like a shroud, and I realized I'd made a foolish mistake. I couldn't live here, a town where Mormon mothers in ankle-length skirts and clunky shoes, their long hair stuffed neatly into buns, wandered through Costco buying up the world, their cunts burning for Jesus, Jesus, only Jesus. Teams of children trailed these mothers, and none of them, not one, neither a mother nor a child, glanced my way. No one saw me. That first week, I stayed with a co-worker at the newspaper, a rooster of a man with a booming voice who always referred to the paper as the "salt mines," and who owned a garage full of kayaks, boats, and bikes that he called his toys. Nothing terribly odd, except how readily he accepted strangers into his house, mostly young men like me, who needed a place to crash before they found an apartment, a rotating harem he supplied with beer and blustery talk. Exactly the type of repressed oddball one finds in towns like Twin Falls, Yakima, Pasco.

I got my own place, a one-bedroom in a sprawling complex with aqua green grass, a pool and exercise room. Not bad, but I was already gone. I had no furniture, just an old futon and piles of clothes, a few dishes. I was drunk by noon on my days off and by midnight on the days I worked the 3-to-11:00 p.m. shift.

One day after work a few of us headed over to the publisher's daughter's place. Gail was funny and sexy with a bit of a belly, nice boobs, frosted blond hair. The best thing, though, was the hot tub stuck in the backyard of the house she shared with this older dude, an ex-con with an actual handlebar moustache, JT. They were just friends, roommates, nothing more, having met at Fridays, where JT tended bar. When two other sportswriters and I arrived at Gail's house, JT pulled out a little baggie of weed, and the five of us smoked around the kitchen table, and I hoped it wasn't my turn to be randomly drug tested by the newspaper that week. Eventually we found ourselves in the hot tub, stoned, telling stories until it was just the boss's daughter and me, side-by-side with warm bubbles tickling our throats. I slid out of my bathing suit and tossed it on the cement where it landed with a satisfying plop. Gail followed with her bikini top as we heard JT's voice booming forth from the kitchen as he described his time incarcerated, how he was never interested in "any hairy bungholes."

"No sir, that ain't me," he shouted. "The old fist worked fine."

"Why's he yelling?" I whispered to Gail.

"I don't know. He talks really loudly when he gets messed up," she said, laughing and rubbing her lovely side boob against my arm, inviting me in, so I reached for her hand to show her what she was doing to me. She touched me for only a moment, smiling, before leaping out and reaching for a towel.

"Where you going?" I asked.

"I'm saving you," she said, turning to me, while wringing the water from her long hair, the towel only around her waist, her fine boobs standing free in the cool night air. "My father would fire a reporter in an instant if he knew they were fooling around with me."

I shrugged. "Maybe I don't care about being fired."

"There's something wrong with you," she said, her hands on her hips, looking like a backwoods Wonder Woman.

"It's just this place," I said. "I mean, what was it like growing up here?"

"Here? How should I know? We moved around a lot when I was a kid, but I think any place is pretty much like any other once you get used to it."

I laughed.

"What?" she asked.

"No, that's exactly what my Irish uncle told me before I moved to Montana. I think he was trying to give me a little life lesson before my big journey West."

"Well, it's true, you know" she said.

"Maybe."

We stared at each other, measuring something.

"C'mon. Why don't you come back in?" I asked.

"No, you're bad," she said, shaking her finger at me, before putting on her shirt and walking back inside.

THE NEXT DAY I drove to the canyon overlooking the Snake River, a deep dive of jagged rock, a big dollop of beautiful in this town of high-desert ugly. I found a wooden bench and tried to cool my brain. I couldn't fathom how this would end. A young couple strolled by, chatting in German, attractive in their tight Euro T-shirts and jeans, eyeing me a moment before switching to English to ask if I'd be kind enough to take their picture standing in front of the scenic overlook—the river nearly six-hundred feet below, twisting blue loneliness, tufts of green along its sides. I snapped their photo, and we talked some. I asked them about the Wall coming down, what that was like, and they told me they were just kids at the time, twelve or thirteen, and it had felt like a game, something that really didn't matter in their lives. This surprised me. They wanted to hear my thoughts on poor Matthew Shepherd. I didn't know what I could say to explain something like that, so I said the usual things. As they were leaving, the man asked to take my picture, so I stood where they had, smiling like they had, my hand on my hip.

They laughed and moved off, the woman calling back, "*Danke. Danke.*"

WHEN I WASN'T DRUNK or working, I often drove to Missoula. One Friday, Jill and I met halfway, in Salmon, Idaho, in a $40 hotel room for a six-pack and a fuck. We stayed the night, in between places, whispering our plans. The carpet was orange, and there was a framed print of a buffalo with ghost eyes above our bed. Jill was headed for an arts residency in Wyoming, and told me, as we parted on that Saturday morning, that her moody-ass brother Simon was living in our big house next to the hamburger joint for the month. It wasn't really my house any longer, but my cat, Reed, was still there, so I drove the three hours to Missoula, and Simon was none too happy to see me. He'd come to town to play chess in coffee shops, to think, to smoke weed, to soak in that one-of-a-kind Missoula vibe. Before I even put down my bag, he told me to get out. We screamed at each other for awhile. He mentioned the cops and stormed upstairs. I left, but not without the TV, my TV, jogging with it to my car, the cord trailing along behind me, sure that Simon would follow and kill me dead. *"Danke,"* I called back as I ran. *"Danke."*

A part of me still jogs along like that, a man scampering down the street carrying his own stolen TV, a looter of his own life, but grateful all the same.

SAN FRANCISCO

IT ENDED WITH AN argument outside a businessman's bar on Van Ness Avenue in downtown San Francisco. Gabe was shouting into the fog, jamming his index finger into the air, his chin pointed right at me, the veins of his neck bulged blue in the city night. We went way back, Gabe and I, all the way to Philly, and I couldn't understand why he was so angry, nor how at the end of that night we would end-up strangers, gone from each other. I still don't.

I'd met Gabe, years earlier, at an art theater in Old City, a shadowy section of Philly where the street lights were refigured gas lamps first used when Franklin and Jefferson roamed the cobblestone streets. The opening credits of Stephen Frears' *My Beautiful Laundrette* flickered across the screen the day Gabe came up to Rita and me to offer his hand in the dark. It felt like yogurt, this shake—cold, slippery and soft. Gabe was working as an usher at the upscale theater, and in his red vest, his gold laminated nametag glimmering in the dark, he whispered a quick hello before shuffling away. It wouldn't surprise me to learn that he'd orchestrated this darkened, rushed introduction so as to avoid the full-on hee-haw, glad-to-know-you formalities upon first meeting someone. And I wouldn't have blamed him.

"He's shy," Rita whispered as he walked away.

"Who isn't?" I said.

For weeks after this meeting, Gabe ignored me. He grew up in the same scrapple-eating neighborhood as Rita, so he often popped in for a visit when I was over at her house trying to settle in with her large clan. This was 1987, and in Gabe's eyes I was just a lowly business major at Drexel University. Gabe, on the other hand, was a budding artist extraordinaire—a painter slash animator slash filmmaker, a genius who slouched around in torn jeans and a pair of Van Gogh's boots, so he didn't exactly warm up to me until Rita gave him something I wrote, an essay/story entitled *Ed McMahon's Laugh* which was published in a zine called *Brain Dead*. It was nothing more than a rant really, an anti-consumerist screech in which I railed against all things corporate, capitalistic, and false, comparing myself to the Beats, "the underground man, the rebel, the mute off-spring of Kerouac and Burroughs dreaming up a new consciousness." Other than its sheer passion, the best thing about the essay was its title, a perfectly employed metaphor (before I really even thought about metaphors) decrying what I found pernicious, unavoidable, and soul-crushing about growing up in America in the 80s. And in the very same issue, Gabe published a one-page graphic story called "There is No Dog," a fragmenting piece of Cold War angst showing, in reverse order, a dead-man's hand reaching for a brick, a soldier's boots, a British flag, a soda bottle with a gasoline-soaked rag stuffed in its top, and a menacing line of soldiers. It read: *There is no dog. The sergeant walked the wall. The young man did not move.* We ate this stuff up back then, so young, so romantic—so sure we knew a better way to live than the rest of the working-class hordes.

But more than art, it was Rita, really, who first drew Gabe and me together. The day I met her, at a party in Connecticut, I'd felt up an orange and imagined it as her, as my summer day, and she'd laughed, saying I reminded her of a friend, Gabe. Not what I wanted to hear from this girl who'd bewitched me from the first moment—earlier in the afternoon in the sun, stoned, listening to The Cure as she strode toward me, smiling, in a white summer dress and Chuck Taylors, to ask, "Do you like The Cure?"

And with that one question, my life with her began.

See, Rita had a face that made men stop in the street, look twice, and make sure it wasn't really Michelle Pfieffer slumming around Philly in a thrift-store coat and an army-surplus shoulder bag. And though she had the same Scandinavian cut to her face as the famous actress—cheekbones like moons, gray eyes, skin as smooth as brushed glass—she wasn't impressed with her own beauty, and she scoffed at the way people expected her to use it. She didn't bother with makeup, tight clothes, and dismissed the idea of motherhood. Eventually, she went away, and I'd give away all these stories, all these sorry words for just a few private ones with her. One talk. An afternoon anywhere.

Instead, I consider this: What drew Gabe to me might have been his love for Rita, a love evident in some photographs he'd taken of her, photographs he'd bought out like a proud parent the first time I visited him at his mother's house, where he lived during college. ("Any nudes?" I'd asked when I'd found out she'd often posed for him. "No," she'd said. "But I'd do it if he asked.") In one print, she'd shaved her head ala Sinead O'Connor and held a shade-less lamp beside her stunning face, leaving one side of it bathed in shadow—the lit bulb and her shaved head caught in a strange muted shadow dance, point/counter-point. Beauty and proportion. It was sublime, this image, one of the most stunning things I'd ever seen. Still is.

But Rita didn't love him, Gabe that is. She loved me, ridiculous little me, and long after she'd left me for that man named Vijay, this love, Rita's dead love for me, had kept us together, Gabe and me—kept us together in Philly and through my moves to Seattle and Montana—and now San Francisco, the end of the 90s, the internet boom, when everyone dreamt of the next big thing, the next web startup that would go public and rake in millions, and anyone with a pulse could find a job with a decent salary and benefits. Even Gabe and I found work. And Gabe even found a girl to go along with his shiny new job, a girl named Dolores, who hated me, I think, because I reminded her of a boy that had broken her heart. But what really doomed us was the simple fact that Gabe had had enough with the art world by then. He'd traded in his frayed, unlaced leather work boots for a pair of polished Doc Martens, clunky and arty, yes, but false, fit for the office, corporate to their very soul. I just don't think he wanted me around any more. Maybe I'd become synonymous with the world he'd spurned, or perhaps he'd begun to see me as an impediment to his new life in San Francisco. Or maybe this animosity stretched back to the beginning when I'd taken Rita away and he'd let me know of his disapproval with that ho-hum shake in the darkened theater.

I don't know, nor will I ever, but it was something like this until we shadowboxed that bad night outside the bar on Van Ness. I'd moved to San Francisco with Jill to be close to my friend, and now here he was begging me to hit him, but I was telling him, no, over and over, no—it wasn't going to happen that way. That bar would be closed in six months, just about the time I'd leave San Francisco forever, but first there was this night, this one bad night.

We'd been drinking in the bar for only a few min-utes, two drinks' worth, before our argument had spilled onto the cold anonymity of Van Ness. I wish it'd been the Castro, or the Mission, or even North Beach, there among the tourists, but it was this nowhere sidewalk of a midtown businessman's bar featuring bonsai trees atop each metal table, couches beneath mirrors along the back wall to make the place look bigger, all of it bathed in the throbbingly useless wail of bad techno. And if there is a sadder sound anywhere than a drum machine bouncing off the mirrored walls of an empty room I hope never to hear it. It was ghastly, and I saw all the ghosts dancing in front of those mirrors, touching their necks shyly, grinning, stealing glances in the near darkness.

"Let's get the fuck out here," Gabe had growled.

I'd followed him outside to face the end of things, a little thrilled with the anger in his voice. I felt it too, that anger, in the back of my throat, and in my heart, and my lungs, and my balls. It seemed we didn't know what to do with each other now that we were finished as friends. The cards had been dealt; our bets made. It was time to show our hands.

EARLIER THAT EVENING, I'D showed up at his apartment to split a celebratory six-pack of Red Stripe. I don't remember ever being with Gabe without drinking, thousands of drinks between us. It was who we were, and we were good at it, and on that night we were toasting his new place. He had just signed a year lease on the apartment and we were drinking beers at his wall of windows, watching a sorry scene play out on the sidewalk in front of his apartment— two drunks arguing until the spinning lights of a patrol car showed up. The cops pulled themselves wearily from their car, their nightsticks hanging from their sides like pelts.

Gabe's new place sat above a Burger King and the smell of the charcoal-flavored meat filled his two rooms. And it was then, as we watched the cops handcuff one of the men, that I heard it for the first time.

"Would you like fries with that?"

I'm sure Gabe had already heard it and was now trying his best to ignore it, but when I heard that amplified drone echo up at us all I could do was let my jaw drop and smile like a goof.

"Are you serious?" I said.

"Thank you for your order, come again," the mechanized voice droned. My mind raced with a kind of sick glee: How many times would Gabe hear that voice? What time did the restaurant close? Did he notice it when he looked at the place? Was that why he'd gotten such a deal on the lease? I grinned, pitying my friend, but I quickly wiped the smile from my face, understanding that Gabe hadn't noticed the voice until he'd signed the lease and moved in.

"Fries with that?" the voice came again.

The laughter bubbled out of me. I couldn't help it. I was an asshole in those days, that's part of this story. I was young and arrogant and still wanted to believe the world couldn't hurt me, owed me something, even though Rita had already torn out my liver and fed it to me.

"Fries with that? Are you fucking serious?" I barked out.

Gabe glared at me. I tried to control myself.

"Don't worry about it," I said. "You'll get used to it."

"Yeah, I'll get used to it. You can get used to a lot of bullshit."

"There you go. Spoken like a true optimist."

What was wrong with us? Why were we playing around with the world like it was a joke? Who did we think we were fooling? What rights did we think we had?

Some answers: We were young. We were fools. We were drunks playing with our lives. In workingman dive bars, in Philly, I'd grin and say, "Look around, there's genius in here," and depending on his mood Gabe would either agree or disagree, loathe or love me, his dear friend and enemy.

We were too much alike, Gabe and me: working-class guys wanting membership into an exclusive club called The Artist. My father had worked for the post office for forty-three years. Gabe's dad, a plumber, had been dead fifteen years when I met Gabe. But we were different from our old men—we were visionaries with something to say. And that was the key, the answer to our riddle, it excused everything, until a few years before Frisco, circa 1997, during my first stint as a sportswriter in Montana, when, with a tall boy between my legs, I was pulled over by a state trooper and asked to kneel before the trooper on the side of the road as if I were about to blow him. And I think I would have, if it'd come down to that or a DUI, but he'd just pulled out a plastic gadget, placed it in my mouth, and told me to blow. I blew, thinking, *body of Christ*, and the trooper said, "You're just under," and I thought, under what, before realizing he meant my blood alcohol content. He allowed me to drive on, but tailed me back into town, waiting for one false move so he could flick on his over-heads and put me in jail for the evening, where I probably belonged.

When I got home that night I was shaking with fear and alcoholic self-pity. A DUI would have meant I couldn't drive and if I couldn't drive I couldn't work and if I couldn't work....To ease my mind, I checked my email. I'd just started up with the e-mail, this new magical mode, and a few days previously, in one of the first emails I'd ever writ-ten, I'd asked Gabe to send me Rita's address. No big deal, I thought. I was thinking I might e-mail her. Why not? Who knew what might happen? This is what happened: That night, there was a returned message from Gabe. He declined to give me her address, the bastard. This enraged me. And still does. I thought it so self-righteous of him. Rita had been gone for six years by then and he'd often tantalize me with stories about her visiting him or talking to her over the phone, and only this once had I ever taken the bait and asked about her, asking if she ever asked about me.

He'd written, cryptically, "Yes, a lot more than you ask about her, but I don't think I can give you her email. It's not a good idea."

When I got Gabe's message, I fired off a reply, blasting him for all his hypocrisies. I can hardly remember what I wrote, but it must have been bad because I don't think he ever forgave me, and it was this message, more than anything else, that led us to that bad night in San Francisco—Gabe jabbing his finger and screaming into the night.

"Fries with that?"

THE PROBLEM IS WE all have so many stories of this type, and I'm afraid they might not add up to much but a sigh and a so what? Yes, they mean something to us, but so what? Consider the strange fact that once, a few years after leaving San Francisco, I decided against a move from Montana to Washington, moving instead from Missoula to Helena. I could have gone to Oak Harbor, Washington—and this decision came after weeks of debate, but the strange truth is while moving my things from Missoula to Helena I'd ended up stuck behind a truck with the words Oak Harbor looped across its roll-up backdoor. The truck, like me, was headed east, and had nothing to do with the actual town of Oak Harbor, but instead was the name of a furniture store. How could that be? What could it mean? Am I talking about God here? Is that all this is—needing God, but not believing in anything but the next day, the next city, the next choice?

·

BUT WHAT I'M TRYING to understand here is the months I spent in San Francisco during the late 90s, and how my time there culminated in that bizarre confrontation with Gabe in front of the bar on Van Ness. We were getting old before the other's eyes, my face aging faster than the rest of my body—the red splotches on my cheeks, always there after a few drinks, began to linger, and my hair was thinning, while my teeth, always bad, were edging toward the grotesque. This in a city of beautiful people—I was no longer beautiful.

I think the actual argument that night started when I spoke against Rita's sister, Sandra, some innocuous comment on which Gabe pounced. I was just drunk, a drunk being a drunk, but this insult touched a nerve in Gabe, or so he acted, taking it as an opportunity to defend Rita's family (and Rita's people were like Gabe's people, the same stock of working-class whites that had hunkered down along the edges of the city for decades as Philly slid into the toilet during the 70s, people who had stayed put, unlike my people, who'd fled to the suburbs at first light). I might also have said something about that in the e-mail I sent the day I was pulled over. I don't know. Maybe if I told it right, if I could speak about the light on the street that evening, how it mingled with the fog and mellowed even Gabe's insane anger. Or maybe this story might make more sense if I set it in front of the Korean restaurant where Gabe and I had eaten the previous week, the place where they supplied you with raw meats and vegetables to cook in a pot over a flame in the middle of a table, huge glasses of imported beer at the ready to wash it all down.

But it didn't happen there.

It happened in front of that nowhere bar on Van Ness,

my friend yelling at me on the sidewalk. The eponymous, gassy groan of the buses, this sound more city than anything I know. The moon there, only glimpsed through the drifting fog.

I don't know.

The truth is I don't know why any of this happened. Have I mentioned the candy-colored Victorians? Have I mentioned the Mexicans I bought weed from in the Mission, or the lovely gay men in the Castro, how they sauntered arm-in-arm so happily, so free that it broke my heart and made me hopeful about the future? And though I've told you that even though this was 1999 and everyone was dreaming of getting rich, I must say I didn't care about money, and that instead of skipping lunch and eating at my desk like all my industrious co-workers, I took long walks at noon, wandering around Union Square in front of the St. Francis Hotel, hoping to bump into the ghosts of Kerouac and Cassidy.

And maybe that was the thing between Gabe and me. The clincher. I still believed in the pursuit of something other than the dollar, still believed it was worth it, that there was a better, more authentic way to live, but he didn't. And maybe all of this is as simple as that. He had his new shoes, his new girl, his new apartment, his new job in his new city, and couldn't be my friend anymore. I was the past, a reminder of all the things he no longer cared about or wanted. What more needs to be said? If I saw him today, I would say only this: Gabe, I believed. I believed in all of it, *the underground man, the rebel, the mute outsider.* I believed every single word.

And I still do.

WHITEFISH

In Whitefish, I finally quit drinking. I could say this quitting had something to do with the majesty of the Rocky Mountains, such open stretches of wonder after that cramped ugly apartment in San Francisco, where we had lived for a few months and where our cat, Jessie, had died. How he died. And it's true, Whitefish was a jewel of a place, a funky ski town at the base of Big Mountain, about as far north as one could go in the continental United States, where I once sat outside on a summer's night watching the Northern Lights pulsate a shower of neon across the sky, but, really, Whitefish had little to do with me quitting the hooch. I stopped because of vanity, the simple fact that drink was causing me to lose my looks. Burst blood vessels in my cheeks had turned my face bloated and ugly. Enough with the booze, I thought one morning, staring into the mirror. Enough.

It went OK for a while. I fell back into the groove of sportswriting—my own writing in the early afternoon, while reporting only at night, when my brain had already tired—but at the beginning of our second year in Whitefish our life sort of broke apart when Jill got a three-week gig teaching on the Rosebud Reservation in South Dakota, a name I thought was surely a joke.

"Rosebud? That's the famous line from Citizen Kane, isn't it?" I asked Jill when she told me she might go there. "Orson Welles whispered it as he died in the movie."

"What? I don't know."

"Yeah, rosebud," I said. "I think it was the name on his sled when he was a kid, and it was meant to symbolize his lost innocence or something."

"Rosebud? That's cheesy."

"That's symbolism," I said.

"Well, I think I should go," she said. "It's decent money. And I love working on the rez."

"OK."

So she went to the Rosebud Reservation, coming home fucked by someone else (some Nebraskan bartender named Chuck who gave her his number on the inside cover of a matchbook). Yes, I found the matchbook, and some emails, and a notebook, and a jagged little piece of me gave way as I got furious and decided (or realized) I couldn't live without her. We screwed like monkeys for a month, sometimes five or six times a day, as I tried to fry that feeling from my insides.

Jill knew she had me within her grasp then, and she knew I knew she knew, and she knew I liked it, so we became like a regular couple—going to movies, dinner, hanging out with friends, friends like Lydia and Mikal, a big-headed bearded lug who'd quit the booze years ago and was now my example of sober good will. It hurt just looking at him. He had once been with Jill, but ditched her, he'd said at the time, because she wasn't on a journey. Like Lydia. But that was a few years back. Now, he and Lydia were happily married, parents of a toddler, while Jill and I were waddling after the same sort of life.

One day, we met them in Missoula and drove up to Seeley Lake together, just the four of us for a day of barbecue, swimming, and talk. Their marriage came up a lot, the actual ceremony, which was performed on the banks of the Big Blackfoot before the wedding party floated down the river on guided rafts. During this float, a frothy wave had pitched one of the guests, an older woman in Tevas and a matronly one-piece, over the side, almost washing her away, but she'd managed to hang on, clinging to a safety rope with some kind of Vulcan death grip. I was right there, sitting next to her on the raft, when it happened. In fact, I was the one who'd pulled her back into the boat, and I can still see the white of her hand holding that rope, how her mottled skin shouted up at me. Help! Even then, while it was happening, I knew there was a lesson in that grip.

"I mean there was no way she was going to let go," I said to the others at Seeley as we sat with our toes in the rocky sand, reminiscing. "It was like Tom Cruise in *Mission Impossible*."

Mikal laughed and reached for Lydia, while Jill reached for my hand. Just about then, a family drove up in a mini-van and piled out, an old woman among them, crouching over her cane as if our talk had somehow summoned her from the pages of memory. She shuffled to the edge of the water to look across, brooding like that, her shoulders pinched until a little girl ran up to her side, her grand-daughter, I suppose.

"I swam across here when I was younger," I heard her tell the child.

The girl thought about it for a long second before saying, "It doesn't look that far."

The old woman laughed and said, "It felt like forever."

That's about all I remember of our Seeley trip.

THE NEXT DAY, JILL and I climbed Jumbo, a mountain overlooking Missoula, which had once, thousands of years ago, been at the bottom of a glacial lake, the whole fucking town once just sediment, silt, muck, and mud. Some dreamers had shaped white rocks into the word *Love* on the side of the mountain, so Jill probably knew what was coming even before I got down on one knee and offered her a tiny blue sapphire that had cost me two weeks' pay. My voice trembled as I asked the question.

She smiled and said, "OK."

This is so cheesy, I thought.

JUST A FEW DAYS after the proposal, maybe a week, Jill told me she was pregnant and that night in Whitefish, after she'd gone to bed, I went to our small yard framed by poplar and spruce trees. Vanilla light gloamed down, cooling me as I smoked and began to cry. I had no idea. Later that week, Jill would truck in two hundred pounds of good dirt from Arlee to start a box garden that she'd water and prune for most of the summer, deep into September, until a few dumbass deer trotted into our yard one morning and ate the whole damn thing down to nub. But that night in the yard, it was all still out in front of us, and even though I sensed weird unknown forces had roped Jill and me together in ways we did not understand, I couldn't think of what else to do. A decision had been made, even if the great scroll were still unrolling. I guessed we would have to leave this place, Whitefish. All of a sudden the job wasn't right. What if we moved back to Philly? What if I moved back to Philly, alone? After a few minutes of these thoughts, I felt watched, threw down my cig, and made my way to our back door, hearing, as I treaded softly, the unmistakable growl of a dog at my back.

"Iris," I said, stopping and looking up at the white moon, "you hush now, you go home."

·

THE NEXT DAY, AFTER a spring rain, we went for a drive and found our baby's name in the sky. It's true. We were cruising in my ancient Saab on the highway near Glacier, the mountains like lost brooding gods, and Jill and I were stumbling through a list of baby names, mostly relatives and writers.

"Margaret, Erin, Toby, Emma," Jill said.

"Elizabeth, Jack, Katherine, Esme," I called back.

"Esme," she said. "Like the Salinger story."

"Yes," I said, hearing the echo of Ted that night in the bar when the man had badgered me about being a Jew and we'd sung out our wannabe names with drunken glee.

Just about then, Jill spotted a rainbow looped across Highway 2 like a gate into a new world.

"Look at that," Jill said, nodding to the colors in the sky. "That's got to mean something."

"Maybe," I said, keeping my eyes on the road. "Maybe."

NOWHERE, NEBRASKA

THIS ENDS IN THE land they call the Midwest—Nebraska, where my last girl, Jill, mother-of-my-children Jill, went and screwed a guy named Chuck (this before she became mother-of-my-children), while I was home in Montana, working, covering a ski race for our small-town newspaper. I discovered this one night when I found her journal as I was digging through her things while killing time before the latest episode of *Survivor*, and what I found in that journal somehow led here, to Nebraska, nowhere Nebraska, where I live now with Jill and the kids, a fact that begs to be recognized as some type of fate.

Let's begin with Jill's schoolgirl's copybook, the one with the checkered red and black cover that she used as a journal. I knew there was no turning back when I picked it up and read what Jill had written in her achingly familiar wavy blue script: *I knew there was no turning back when I heard the rip of the condom package.* Reading this, an electric blue thrill tickled itself up from my groin into my belly and finally my throat, charging me up like a windup toy as I stood there dumbfounded, mouth catching flies there in that ranch-style yellow house we shared in Whitefish, down the road from Big Mountain, a high-end ski resort where in summer you could hike trails laced with wild flowers and sage. A lake was within walking distance, deer grazed in our backyard, but what did I feel at that moment? I have no idea, really, but now understand it as my life cracking open, like an egg or a peanut, my future sprinting away like a freed prisoner, and me behind, ready to give mad chase, my cock twirled like a lasso.

First stop: the shitter, reading on while wanking off, not sure why I was so excited—*he picked me up in his clunker of a truck and told me he wanted to show me where he went to high school. High school? I thought. Who is this guy?* I found his name (the aforementioned Chuck—fucking Chuck, upchucking Chuck, Chuck and duck, Lucky Chuck, Chuck, oh fuck), his occupation (bartender), and where it happened, a place called Valentine, a name that gave me some hope, not believing the irony of it until I checked the map and sure enough there it was—Valentine, Nebraska, just south of South Dakota and the Rosebud Reservation, where Jill had gone for a month to work as an Artist in the Schools, a month I'd spent covering state basketball in Columbus Falls, girls tennis in Kalispell, and the U.S. Olympic ski trials on Big Mountain, where Bill Johnson, a former gold medalist vying for a comeback at age 40, had crashed face-first during a training run and had to be airlifted from the mountain, his brain crushed, to say nothing of his dreams. I'd interviewed Johnson two months before his crash, and he'd been so full of big talk and bluster, brashly predicting another gold, sure that everything would turn out his way. How else could it?

OK, one thing at a time, I thought. Shit. Shit. Shit.

I knew I had to get out of that house, so I fed the cat and fled to Columbus Falls, at the lip of Glacier National Forest, loamy and huge, a place where one could disappear. I considered, for a moment, driving over the pass on the road called Going to the Sun, but instead pulled to the side of the road at McDonald Lake and got out of the car and walked to the shore. It was late, the stars were just starting to bloom, and the rocks beneath my feet were gray and smooth to the touch. I picked one up and skipped it into the middle of the lake, the ripples catching the moon's light. On the other side of the mountain waited Cut Bank and Browning, the Blackfeet and Blood Indians, Canada.

I turned around and hightailed it into a grocery store where a toothless clerk eyed me as I felt up some fruit under the sadness of fluorescent light. I found an orange to my liking, paid for it, and walked beaten back to my beater Saab, rusty and worn, where I sat, peeling the fruit, eating it, searching for something to cool my brain, some synchronicity, calling up my first night with Rita—an orange there, my little speech about how I'd wished Rita were this orange so I might peel her. I rejoiced in memory, in the tart juice of it on my tongue, wondering, as I sat in my shitty Saab, if I had the balls to drive away and start my life over yet again.

And if a life can pivot on a single choice, here's where mine did just that. I decided to stay. I wasn't twenty-five anymore, I reasoned. My dad was an old man, he couldn't nurse me through another heartbreak, and I felt too weak to be alone, so I returned to Whitefish (Jill was still not home, still teaching her yoga), fed the cat again (Reed had a nasty thyroid condition that forced him to eat and shit, shit and eat) and sat back down on the shitter, this time grunting one out. And it was while shitting this shit, as fear throbbed through my intestines, that I hatched my plan, the rest of my life. I would ask Jill to marry me and give her what she wanted—a baby.

But first I had to spend the night at a Super 8, pretending (to myself) that I hadn't made such a decision. It was a long night. I wished for the booze, but I'd already buried that part of me, so I sat on my bed surfing the tube, settling on an old Hitchcock, *The Trouble with Harry*, and wore myself down to sleep, hoping I wouldn't dream. But I did—of Rita, lovely Rita, coming to me with hot chocolate and words. We collapsed into bed and made love before she drove away.

When morning came, so did Jill. She found me, my door. Knocked. I let her in, and after some sorry business, we fucked like teenagers on the bed of that budget hotel, this fucking the first of many such fucks as spring leaked into lush Rocky Mountain high summer. My marriage proposal came later, in June, in Missoula, on the side of a mountain where white rocks had been gathered to spell out the word *Love*, the L bigger than the rest of the letters, big enough to be seen from downtown. The locals called it Love Mountain.

But before I proposed, Jill and I took a trip to Albuquerque in May trying to figure ourselves out. It was hot, hot, hot. We visited Pueblo villages, ate spicy pizza, hiked mountains adorned with rock carvings thousands of years old, and, of course, continued to fuck like bunnies, as if we were trying to stave off the death of us. When we'd first arrived, as we drove from the airport in our rental Ford pickup (white as the snow in Whitefish), Jill dipped down in the seat and gave me a mind-bending blowjob as cars zipped past us on the highway—a blowjob, that even in memory, still gives me wood.

What happened between Jill and me during that spring and summer when we did so much fucking and fighting relates back to my fear of being alone (I'm no different than you) and the fact that I was enflamed, inspired, if that's the right word, by some other guy fucking Jill, my Jill, and I went sort of batty with jealousy. I broke two phones, threw a table against a wall, punched said wall, and smoked and smoked and smoked. Jill started a garden. She had two hundred pounds of good dirt delivered to our driveway, a day when, if my calculations are correct we conceived our first child, our lovely daughter Esme, though Jill likes to think this happened up on Big Mountain, among the wildflowers. And if there's any type of heroism in this story it's that I kept out of my cups, so the nights were long (and full of smoke) and not being able to put myself to sleep with alcohol, I stayed up asking my questions. Jill, foolish girl, answered them all.

Did you come? (No.)

Did he come? (Yes.)

How long did it last? (Not long? Maybe ten minutes.)

Did you like it? (No, it kind of hurt.)

Were you wet? (No, and he moved really fast. I don't think he'd slept with a lot of girls.)

Did you keep your clothes on? (Yes.)

Did he? (No, nothing but his socks.)

Where did you place your hands while he fucked you? (I don't remember.)

Did you touch his ass while he fucked you? (No.)

What was his body like? (He was really muscular and bald.)

How old was he? (Twenty-six.)

All this was like tearing out my liver, salting it, and then devouring it. Painful, but delicious, as honest as two people can ever be.

Eventually, we made it to Maine, the wedding there, where no one but my father guessed my game. Dad cried himself to sleep the night before I was married, the night of our reception dinner, when I arrived in a fancy print shirt with blue palm trees swaying in the breeze. When Dad saw that shirt, he'd said, "That's not you," and he was right, just as the goatee I grew to hide behind was not me.

A few years later, as my father lay dying, we went back

to New Mexico, our little daughter in tow, and tried to recapture something of what it felt like to be jealous and in love, and a little bit crazy. It didn't really work. We ran out of money and the police came to our door to make sure we could cover our bill. And after this, when I finally made it home to Dad's bedside (two weeks before he would fall down cellar steps and split open his skull and die), Dad had asked me about this second trip to New Mexico. He had no time for bullshit, but I couldn't really explain why we'd gone to that steamy orange desert where the mountains rivaled Montana's. I couldn't really explain how we were out chasing an older version of ourselves, couldn't explain how there are people in the world like us, fools and dreamers, weak-kneed motherfuckers who believe if you look hard enough you might just find the threads connecting your life, threads that hold us together at the same time they threaten to split apart.

THE SUBURBS

I FOUND HIM ON my sister's back deck—mid-July, humid, the cicadas humming, the *Philadelphia Daily News* splayed across his lap, his eyes liquidy and weird, nearly as wide as half-dollars.

"Stew, what are you doing here?" he asked.

I shrugged. I'd driven from Nebraska to Philly on my way to Maine, where my pregnant wife and in-laws waited. Almost immediately that day, Dad dispensed with the small talk and began telling me about his dream. He'd just returned from Pennsylvania Hospital at 9th and Locust where they'd cut open his belly to clip out the cancer there, but they hadn't been able to get it all out.

"In the margins," my sister had told me. "They left some in the margins."

This, we all knew, was a death sentence.

Dad told me that while he was in post-op he'd dreamt the nurse caring for him was the devil. And in this dream, my younger brother Jason, now a doctor living in Florida with his second wife, was waiting to meet Dad at the corner bar (or the tappie, as my father called it). Jason was watching a prize fight on TV as he waited (a Tyson fight, Dad said, and I remembered the Douglas-Tyson fight with the beefy underdog Douglas stalking Tyson around the ring, shocking the champion and the world by knocking out Iron Mike, a fight Dad and Jason had indeed watched together), and apparently, it was while dreaming this dream—Jason waiting down at the tappie—that Dad had torn out his IVs and wandered the hospital's hallways, ending up in a janitor's closet where they found him the next morning sitting on an upturned bucket, muttering his curses.

"I think I was looking for that bar," my dad said.

After this they had someone sit with Dad 24/7.

"It was probably just the morphine," my dad half chuckled in that dismissive way of his. "But I was convinced my nurse was following me around with a long needle, trying to jab a needle in my neck, right next to the bone there."

Dad tapped the inside part of his clavicle.

"Your clavicle," I said.

"Yeah, whatever—my collarbone," he said. "My neck. He was trying to kill me, you understand, and the next thing I knew I was in that janitor's closet."

Dad had told his story to at least a half-a-dozen people, varying the details slightly with each telling, but every story was warm with the same wicked urgency—talk not meant to impress or illicit a chuckle, but words born from the need to elude, to get past, to get out. He had slipped down the rabbit hole of his own death and was scratching around for an escape. I'm going to die, he was telling everyone with this story—I'm going to die and I don't understand, but you might help by listening. We listened, of course, hoping he was wrong, but knowing he wasn't, and I thought of Scheherazade, how, like her, Dad was trying to save himself for one more day.

HE WAS DEAD WITHIN a month, and a few months after that I was headed to Boothwyn to clean out his house, the home where I'd grown up, which had sat untouched since his death. Texas was playing USC in the Fiesta Bowl the night I flew into Philly, and since cable was out at Dad's, I'd booked a room downtown, telling myself I wanted to watch the game, when, really, I just didn't want to arrive exhausted from my flight and have to drive a rental car to my boyhood home to deal with ghosts at that hour.

Sure enough, the airline lost my luggage, so by the time I finally made it into the city I was behind schedule, rushing, disorientated. I circled the city blocks until I found an overnight garage, parked my rental, and set off on foot for The Alexandrian, a boutique hotel somewhere between 12th and 13th on Spruce Street, still hoping to catch the second half of the game. Walking from the garage to my boutique hotel, it began to snow, and I recalled another winter day a few years ago, when just a block south on Sansom Street—an almost lover, a suitor, Robert—a tall, elegant man who called himself an actor, rose up on his toes and spun in the middle of a deserted street as the light of the day waned around him. He might even have been singing. I don't remember exactly, so many of the gay men I knew in those days often broke out into impromptu song, but I do know he was dancing in the snowy street, drunk and happy, and I had watched, laughing, alive to the muffled silence of the falling snow, the soft patterns of our footprints trailing down the street, the flecks of snow cold on my cheeks.

Robert and I were fresh from Houlihan's, an upscale margarita bar next to a dive bar, McGlitchey's, where I'd split my fair share of cheap pitchers of Rolling Rock with my college buddies, bookishly reciting Keats while planning never-to-happen road trips to Mexico and Alaska, times that even back then, with Robert, had seemed like a lifetime ago. That day in the street, Robert and I had been scheduled to work a party at the Frog, the catering company where we both eked out a living, but the snow had canceled the party, so naturally we'd headed to Houlihan's for a late-afternoon cocktail or two. At the time, they were filming the movie *Philadelphia* in town, and Denzel Washington had been spotted drinking at Houlihans, though no one ever saw Tom Hanks. Hanks was probably too busy rehearsing his big scene in the movie, his head-swaying dance across the hardwood floors of a fancy loft apartment as he trailed along his IVs and listened to Italian opera, a scene that felt trumped up and phony from the first moment I saw it. People I knew danced when they were drunk or happy, not when they had IVs hanging from their arms, not when they were dying. My father certainly didn't dance before pulling out his IV and heading to that janitor's closet. There was no opera playing, just him in the dark, muttering his curses on an upturned bucket as he tried to find a bar to watch a fight.

"He put the needle in and then he waited," Dad had said. "He had this look on his face, this little smile. I had to fight my way out. I had to get to the corner tappie because Jason was there. He was watching the Tyson fight."

"In Tokyo," I said.

"What?"

"In Tokyo. Douglas-Tyson. That's where the fight was."

Dad shrugged, went on with his story.

Now, a few months later, I was hurrying to my boutique hotel to make the second half of a football game, thinking of Robert twirling on Sansom Street—his funny baritone. I'd always liked Robert, liked his efforts at dignity, liked how he always tried to make me laugh. Lost in my little reverie, I had taken a wrong turn only to find myself in front of the shabby motel where Robert had rented a room by the month, and standing there looking up at the crumbling brick façade of that building, that snowy late afternoon in the street returned in full force, how when we'd arrived at his motel he'd tried to convince me to go up to his room for a drink. He'd pointed up to single lit window that he said was his, and asked, "One drink?"

I hesitated. He pirouetted in the street, and asked again, "Just one drink?"

I was lost then, I realized. Holding a receipt with the boutique's address scrawled on the back, I went into the lobby of Robert's old motel to ask the clerk if he could help. The floors were dirty, the sofa torn, and the walls covered by faded green wallpaper trimmed in tacky gold. At the counter, a group of three squawking drunks held court, no clerk in sight, while in a corner chair, an old man sat reading the *Daily News*. Dad? I thought as the desk clerk emerged from a back room, ignoring us all as he spoke into his cell.

That afternoon with Robert, I'd rebuffed his advances, but had agreed to a drink in the bar next to the lobby, the same bar I could see into right then as I waited for the clerk to finish his call. A line of sorry drunks sat staring down into their drinks and I knew there was a chance that one of them might be Robert, still there, still waiting.

"Just one drink?"

In the street, he'd kicked out his legs like Baryshnikov, the snow dusting his shoulders as if this were *The Dead*, but as charmed as I was, he was just too old for me, about as old as I am now, with my gray speckled beard, but I did finally agree to a drink, and as I did I wondered exactly how many drinks it would take for me to go upstairs with him.

I left in the middle of my third when I'd felt some tipping point approaching.

THREE NIGHTS LATER, THE cleanup at my dad's house done and getting ready to head back to Nebraska on a flight tomorrow, I was on the phone with my wife Jill when someone knocked on the door. It was late, too late for anyone to be knocking on the door of a dead father's suburban home. I was prepared to leave early the next morning, never to see this place again.

"Don't answer it," Jill said over the phone.

How could I not answer it? In a way, this was the end of my boyhood, maybe the last person knocking up to see if I were home, to see if I wanted to come out and play. Maybe it was my best friend from across the street, also named Stewart, back from Texas, where he had moved when I was twelve, back to see if I wanted to ride our bikes around the block. Or maybe it was my father, Scrooge-like, back from the dead for a surprise visit.

"Hello?" I called out.

AFTER THOSE TWO AND half drinks with Robert in the lobby bar that afternoon, he walked outside with me, and again, on the sidewalk there, asked me up to his room.

"We don't have to do anything," he said, perhaps one of the saddest things anyone has ever said to me.

"Sorry," I said. "I can't."

All this, because Robert, like everyone at the Frog, knew I'd fooled around with Darrell a few months earlier, during a party at his place. He'd cornered me in a laundry, Darrell did, before he lifted me onto a washer, and taken me out of my pants. He'd sucked my cock right there, right then, the noise of the party leaking through the laundry room's flimsy sliding door until that door had slid open and the only other straight man at the party had stuck his head in and said, "Oops! Sorry. I didn't know anyone was in here."

Oops, sorry.

But Robert wasn't Darrell, young, good-looking Darrell, with his muscular torso and ironic banter. Robert had that silly old-man beard and small disturbing cuts around the edges of his lips. Otherwise, he looked OK, and he was funny and tender with his baritone, his actorly ways, but it just wasn't going to happen. I wouldn't let it—I knew if I'd open that door I'd slip too far away from myself, and it would become more than a game, more than me measuring my desire like liquid into a beaker during a high school science experiment, and when Robert realized this, his face registered a look of infinite sadness, a look that mirrored my father's that last week of his life when he was telling me his story of nurse as devil.

THAT NIGHT AT THE Alexandrian, I'd settled into my room with a chocolate shake and a Wendy's grilled chicken sandwich to watch the football game, trying, unsuccessfully, to fight off Dad's story, how one nurse I talked to when Dad was in post-op did sound mean—maybe she was his devil—but the others seemed fine, especially Ron, who seemed to like my father, calling him by his full name, "Phillip." I realized Dad's hospital was only a few blocks away from my boutique, literally around the corner from Robert's residential motel, and that's the Bermuda triangle of this story: boutique, motel, hospital, and how all this happened, years apart, but within a few blocks. Watching the game, however, I became transfixed by Vince Young loping down the sidelines, and forgot about Robert and my father, tasting only my chocolate shake, creamy and sweet atop the salt of the chicken, and for a few warbling moments I was free inside the moment, a hermit in his cave—and just as happy.

THE DAY I LEFT Philly for Maine, Dad fell and hit his head. When they got him to the hospital, he needed an operation to relieve the swelling in his brain. But he was already dying from cancer, we reasoned—what would be the point of the operation? "Why fix the tire of a car with a broken engine?" the surgeon had asked, and we'd nodded our heads like zombies. We did this. This is what happened.

After he fell, after we didn't operate, after they took out my father's breathing tube, I was the first one to arrive, still flushed from a run. When my father saw me, he pulled me close and with great effort raised his head from his pillow and whispered urgently into my ear as I leaned close to hear.

"What is it, Dad? What is it?"

"Home," he said. "Home."

I nodded and lied.

"We'll get you home," I said. "I promise. Home."

LATER THAT NIGHT IN the hotel, I woke to thoughts of my father and voices in the street just below my room. Maybe my father thought that when I'd visited him at my sister's house I was there to save him, but instead I'd ushered in the end.

AT THE BOUTIQUE THE next morning I awoke to find the magic gone. I had to get home; I had a job to do. My luggage was still lost at the airport, my dad was still dead, and Robert just a memory, but it didn't matter. The fact that my boutique hotel was around the corner from Robert's motel and Dad's hospital, didn't matter. I hadn't gone up to Robert's room that night and this was all a game in my head. When I looked at the facts in the cold light of morning, they were trivial, something to ignore. But I can't lie—the thought lingered that I was missing something, that maybe if I'd found the right door, I could slip through a portal and go back to that night with Robert twirling in the street, my father still alive, and I'd still have the choice to spend the night with him, Robert. And maybe that's all I wanted. A choice. Again. Maybe I should have gone up to his room. Maybe we would have done something, maybe not. And maybe we should have allowed the operation, maybe not. Maybe it would have prolonged my father's suffering, maybe not. And maybe, now, I am the middle-aged man with the beard, and maybe through this portal Dad's still trying to tell his story, the same story I'm trying to tell here, the magical one that tricks time, stops it for a moment, the only one worth telling, because after we refused the operation, my father didn't die, not right away as the doctors had assured us he would.

THE PREVIOUS EVENING, WHEN I'd checked into the boutique, my key hadn't worked, so I'd gone down to the clerk for help, and while he went upstairs to fix the problem, I'd waited below, noting another old man in a lobby. Everywhere, old men waiting in lobbies. This one sat leisurely on a small sofa, his feet barely reaching the ground. He was a tiny man, the size of a big boy, and I was confused because my father had been a giant, but of course, I thought, that's what death does—it reduces us all. Dad asked where I was from, and I told him Nebraska, and a funny look spread across his face before I quickly said I was originally from Philly, home visiting my parents. I didn't want to get into the business of Dad's death with Dad, not here, not at this hotel. It was none of his business, really. And I didn't want Dad to tell me how his parents were dead, nor how, these many years later, he still missed them. I'd heard all that before, and I didn't want to hear how important it was to visit when you can still visit. Really, all I wanted to do was to get up into my room, turn on the TV, and settle down with my chicken sandwich and chocolate shake to watch the game.

But old men like to talk, and someday I'll be an old man in a lobby, so when Dad asked how often I made it home, I told him once a year. He smiled and said my parents must be happy to see me.

"Yeah," I said, and our conversation sort of died there, right then, as I wondered why we had to play this game, Dad and I. The football game was on in the lobby too (it was a big game!) and we went quiet and watched it, and it was a little bit like the old days, watching the game with my dad. I wondered what was keeping the clerk. After a minute or two, Dad told me he was originally from Texas, but he had no hint of an accent, and I began to think the man was drunk or just crazy, just the type of man to hang around lobbies and talk to strangers. I told the guy I was rooting for USC just to shut him up.

The clerk finally returned and told me my door was fixed.

"Occasionally, they stick," he said.

"Is it safe?" I said. "I mean I won't lock myself out or anything, will I?"

"You're safe," the old man said, but the clerk ignored him.

"Oh, you just have to wiggle it a little," the clerk said. "It's no problem."

Still, I didn't like it, but the old man scoffed and shook his paper impatiently. The clerk said it was the only room available, "take it or leave it."

I took it. I went upstairs and everything was fine until I was asleep and dreamt that I was stuck in that room, pounding on the door, madly trying to open it, tricking the handle one way then the other. The old man from the lobby was in there too with me, in my dream, in my room, looking over my shoulder as I frantically turned the knob, disagreeing with my efforts.

"Not that way, the other way, clockwise, the way you tighten a screw. You know how to tighten a screw don't you?"

The truth was Dad and I didn't get along too well at times. Sometimes, he doubted my choices, sometimes I almost hated him. And then the man in my dream was on the other side of the door, in the hallway, laughing mockingly through the door, saying, "Sorry, sorry."

I woke up to voices, and then a crashing—a trash can lid rolling down the alley. I knew, instantly, it was my father outside rooting around, and I felt silly in my sadness, my fear about life without my father, and wondered where my luggage was right then, probably on some tarmac in Chicago or St. Augustine or Atlanta.

I couldn't get back to sleep, so I climbed out of bed and went to the window. On the street below, three women stood talking to two men. A few minutes later, the two men left. It was 3:16 a.m.—all the bars had closed. I thought of Robert again, remembering him all over as this story bloomed in my head. I remembered how Robert and I had slipped into the bar down the street, how sad he'd looked when I told him no. Why hadn't I'd just said yes? It would have made him so happy, and maybe me too. His sadness matters, even today, but his sadness is not what this story is about.

I checked the door to my room, popping it open. Just the silent hallway, the gray carpet. I was sure I wouldn't be able to sleep now, so I went back to the window to watch what would unfold. Maybe this was the end of my father's dream. There was a convenience store open on the corner and one of the women disappeared into it, and then two new men came staggering down the street and another of the women followed, leaving only the one, who wore a short, electric-blue dress and no coat. She must be cold, I thought. A car pulled to the curb and this last woman went to the window of this car, a big car, a tan Buick. The guy behind the wheel laughed. I wanted to do something illicit. I took out my cock and stroked it, but I couldn't get hard. I felt too old for all of that now, so I put myself away and just watched—a man in a window looking down at a street. I'd become an Edward Hopper painting. Me, the one writing this. The woman following the two men had followed them into an alley, but they were just talking by some trash cans. I wanted her to dip her head below and take one of the men into her mouth. Or I wanted her to be raped, something obscene, with me upstairs, maybe calling the cops, maybe not. The hero or the villain. But nothing like that happened. The scene played itself out, almost listlessly. The woman talking to the Buick disappeared into it. The one who had gone into the store came out with cigarettes and stood smoking until the one in the alley returned and joined her. They smoked together and laughed. I could hear their voices but not their words. They were both wearing white coats with fake fur collars. They looked like sisters.

"Dad?" I asked.

At the end, after my dad made it out of the University of Pennsylvania alive, after I'd visited him at my sister's, after I left for Maine, after he fell down the steps in my sister's basement, smacking his head flush against the cement floor, after the paramedics screamed in and took him away, after they tubed him, but did not operate to relieve the swelling in his head, after they took out the breathing tube and tied his ankles and wrists to the bed rails and let him lay like that for a number of twenty-three days, they put him on a morphine drip to die. He died like that. That's all. That's what this is about. A son watching his father die, knowing he had an active hand in that death. That's what happened. This is the real end to my father's story, and maybe that's what he saw when he looked at me that day I arrived at my sister's house, the grim reaper huffing in from Nebraska, maybe that's why his eyes were as big as half dollars. It's certainly why I tell this story now.

"Dad?" I said.

In those three weeks, they put these big white mittens on Dad so he couldn't get at his IV lines, but before he completely lost it, he would flop around on his bed, his hospital gown sliding away to show his shriveled cock.

Dad?

Global Aphasia they told us. This is what Dad had, the inability to use or understood language.

That night in the boutique hotel, I watched as a Jeep pulled up to the two women in the fake fur collar jackets leaning against the wall smoking. One of the two climbed into the car and drove away, leaving again only one. She began to play with the zipper of her jacket, zipping it up and down, up and down. I watched her for about ten minutes.

Look up, I thought, just look up.

I thought about going below and offering her a bed to sleep in, asking if she wanted to come up to visit. I realized I could do this, that she would just ask me for money and then it would be a thing happening. We could couple, maybe fuck, whatever, or we could just talk. Years ago, I would have done exactly this. Instead, a man came up to her and there was short, quick argument, and then he was gone. The woman was again alone as I watched, and then a limousine came and she laughed and climbed in like she had won something. The limousine took her away, and I

was left looking down at the empty street almost happy.
Everyone was gone. It was 3:55 a.m. on January 9, 2006. I
was not yet forty, just a child, really, in the grand scheme
of things. I didn't know what I was waiting for, and then I
realized I was waiting for him, my father, streaking down
the street in his hospital gown, his legs grown thin, his
balls flopping free from the gown.

"Dad?" I said.

THREE NIGHTS LATER AT Dad's empty house, Jill still on
the phone, someone still knocking on the front door, Jill
still telling me not to answer it, I went and answered it.
It was a short man in a uniform with a nametag. Ron, the
tag said. Expect the ordinary, they say, because that is what
usually happens. This, too, is the truth.

"Stewart Simmons?" Ron asked.

"That's me."

"Here's your bag. Just sign here"

I signed with a big X. He just looked at me for a hard
second before he shook his head, chuckled, thanked me,
and left.

Back on the phone, I told Jill my bag had arrived.

"Perfect timing," she said. My flight back to Nebraska
was at 8:00 a.m. the next morning. I would never come
back here. I would never see my father again, nor the inside
of this house.

"Do you think I should have tipped him?" I asked Jill.

"No, they lost the bag," she said. "He didn't deserve a tip"

I agreed with her, but didn't say that in the millisecond
between turning the knob and pulling open the door, I was a
boy again, my best friends were waiting, and when I stepped
outside to play no one would catch me. I'd hide and never
be found. I'd run faster than all my friends, throw farther,

yell louder. I would live for centuries, forever, telling stories, this one, until the one coming for me forgot, until I was safe again in my boyhood, in this house—forgiven and alive and laughing.

TOKYO

JULIA AND I LIVED in South Philly, in what the locals
called a trinity, an 18th-century brick house with three
rooms pancaked above a basement kitchen where bars
lined the windows and the ceiling was low enough to
scratch the top of a tall man's head. A spiral staircase
thumbscrewed from the top floor to the basement. I'd
taken one look at the place, my bags still in Julia's car,
and knew I'd go crazy if I stayed longer than a couple of
months.

"This is cool," I said. "This'll work."

Julia had just picked me up from the airport terminal
after my thirteen-hour flight from Tokyo, where I'd gone
to live with my banker brother to teach English for a year
and re-invent myself only to come back, lamely, after six
short weeks. Before I'd fled Japan, I'd caught a fever, moped
around, visited ghostly Kyoto and tribal Korea, where I'd
bought a hand-carved wooden joker's mask, sensing that
I was leaving behind exactly what I'd hankered after for
years—a fresh start, an adventure, a new me. Life in Japan
surely would have blossomed if I'd simply stuck it out. But
I didn't. I couldn't. I'd already punched my ticket home,
already told my brother I was leaving, so I'd gone to a park
and buried a note under a cherry tree, promising myself
that someday I'd be back to dig it up.

I've never gone back, and probably never will, but I like
to imagine this other me, maybe still there, settled down
with a Japanese wife and raising biracial beauties, digging
sumo wrestling, baseball, and the simplicity of tea.

·

I'D RUN INTO JULIA at an AIDS dance benefit a couple of months before I'd left for Japan and shortly after my bad break with Rita, lovely Rita, whom I'd lived with for a cozy five years until April 1, the day (and night) she didn't come home from work, my whole life since then like some kind of hidden-camera April Fools' joke, and a milligram of me still expecting even now, years later, Rita to pop into the room and scream "Gotcha!"

But this story is about Julia. She'd wooed me home with a series of long, breathless phone calls, phone calls which, because of the thirteen-hour time difference, always took place either late at night or insanely early in the morning, and always, always started with the same set of questions: "What are you doing? Are you up? What time is it there?" as if we couldn't believe time could bend like that. These calls had infuriated my brother, who'd presented me the bill, red-faced, while we stood in the Narita airport waiting for my departure flight back to Philly. I'd paid him with the last of my yen, glad to be rid of that money, and not surprised at his attitude—this the guy who had once showed up at my dorm in Philadelphia, red-faced, clutching two twenties, which he shoved into my hands, saying, "You can't call Dad every time you need something, Stewart. You have to learn how to take care of yourself." The very same guy who, years later, would convince me to turn away from my father as he lay dying in the hospital after falling down the basement steps of my sister's house. My father would need surgery to stop the bleeding in his brain and save his life, a surgery we would refuse because at the time he would also be dying (just more slowly) from pancreatic cancer. I would shamefully cede the decision to my older brother, letting my father slip into that dark current as my brother whispered into my ear, "You have to take your emotion out of a decision like this, Stewart. Right? You understand this, yes?"

Julia, though, saved me from all this—Japan, my indecision, myself. She was a sculptress who worked with clay, an artist, the real kind who created objects of beauty, not like me, a sad-sack writer who called himself an artist but scribbled only nonsense, lies, no one would ever read. She had a studio in Old City, and actual people paid actual money for the stuff Julia made—life-sized limbs and torsos, quirky salt-n-pepper shakers molded into the shapes of animals that sold for fifty bucks a pop at craft stores along trendy South Street. I loved her because of her art and because the evidence of this art was everywhere—the front of her jeans, the tips of her finger, her neck.

And soon enough the evidence was in our house, our tiny gingerbread house, where on the first floor a huge, clunky piece of clay shaped into the form of a female torso sat like some demented God, some sliced-apart Buddha. We used it as a side table and called it good. The second floor was not much bigger than a closet, but Julia insisted I make it my study, and I threw myself into this idea with the abandonment of a banshee, working atop a wooden door I'd scavenged from a junkyard in North Philly, hacking away day after day at some new version of myself that, even then, I suspected might take me away from Julia.

IRONICALLY, THE FIRST TIME I'd met Julia I was with Rita at a party in West Philly. Rita was taking one of Julia's pottery classes, maybe because she was sensing my frustration with her orderliness, her perfection, and at this party, in the middle of January, in a bombed-out section of West Philly, there was drinking everywhere, pierced people smoking, a thrash band thrashing, and a back porch where all the badass creative types hung, talking the talk, shivering and smoking under a moonless gray city sky.

I'd ditched Rita, and her exquisite blonde looks, two minutes inside the front door, and headed to the back yard, hoping to find Julia, but really what I sought was myself, that version of me that I wanted to become, the artist, the creative man, anything but the man I was at that moment, saddled in a relationship with a girl who didn't create (or drink), but programmed computers and acted rationally, day after day after day after day. I was twenty-four, two years out of college, unemployed, the first Bush was still in the White House, and I had no clue how to give birth to this idea of myself that I'd been carrying around like a secret, like a boy carrying a frog in his pocket, but on the porch that night I spotted Julia and felt the first scratchings of this new me clawing to get out. Julia had short spiky blonde hair—pretty, but in a butchy sort of way, and she had what looked to be an acorn pinned like a medal to the front of her jean jacket. I sidled up next to her in the moonlight chill and asked for a cigarette. She didn't smoke, but bummed me one from some other guy, and a light too, and we laughed at this, bonding over our role reversals.

When she asked what I did, I said I was a writer. And when she asked what I wrote about, I said, "My generation, you know, how we live in the shadow of the 60's. It's kind of sad how we're not defined and all."

It felt like the truth, and, more importantly, Julia didn't smirk, or laugh, but nodded like I made perfect sense, and when I asked her what she did, she said she was an artist, and right then I wanted her. I remember specifically wanted to exchange Rita, my Michelle-Pfieffer look-alike girlfriend from Roxborough, with Julia, this butch-looking artist in jeans and a denim jacket that matched mine. Rita came outside then, wide-eyed, a little shocked at the scene, and said she wanted to go home, so we went home to fight about it, beginning our mad march away from one another. So nine months later, Rita gone, I'd spotted Julia at the dance benefit in the city, and it seemed like serendipity—it seemed only natural to saunter up and speak to her, kick-starting a relationship even though I was already planning to skedaddle to Japan in two short months. What I didn't know at the time, or what I didn't want to believe (and maybe still don't) is that there is no one directing all of this nonsense, no man behind the curtain directing the way; it's just us and our choices, our silly little choices.

JULIA AND I TRIED to make a life in that house, and for a short time we did. At my junkyard desk, I scribbled my lies, slowly untwisting them, making them a little more true each day. I'd read somewhere that if a person could simply sit still for an hour or two each day and write that by the end of a year's time the routine would have either burned itself inside that person or that same individual would realize the writing life was not the one he wanted. Julia had no such questions. She worked at her studio in Old City, molding her funky women's torsos, her amputated limbs, her lumpy moon rocks, her salt-'n-pepper shakers, her single eyeballs looking right down into the center of me, firing them in a kiln nearly as big as our bedroom, and when I visited her at this studio we often took a six-pack of Rolling Rock to the tarpapered roof that overlooked Old City.

On the roof we bullshitted about love and art, the shiny city below ours, our future itself roaming along the cobblestone streets, slipping past the ghosts of Franklin and

Jefferson, skirting the shadows of the street lamps, our talk, our words, drizzling down on them like rain.

"Where do you want to be in five years?"

"Published. A book. I want a book."

"You can't be in a book. Where do you want to live, Stewart?"

"I don't know. Here. There. I'm not sure it matters. I guess I live mostly in my head, anyway. It's sort of the same everywhere."

"Is that what it was like in Japan, like here?"

"Not at all. There was a whole different way of looking at things over there, a completely different paradigm."

"But how does that make sense if it's the same everywhere."

"Well, amend that. What I'm saying is it's a mindset— East versus West, but within those broader categories things are pretty much the same."

"But don't you get to define those categories, choose your *paradigms*."

"Nice word."

"I know. A little birdie whispered it to me."

"Yeah, well, maybe. I don't know. I think we need more beer."

"I can't. I have to fire a piece in the kiln before we take off."

"What body part is this?"

"Ha. It's a hand with a little bit of the wrist attached, like someone reaching up through the sand."

"What sand?"

"Beach sand."

"What's wrong with dirt?"

"Too ghoulish."

"I want it to be playful. I want people to laugh."

"Dirt isn't funny?"

"You want dirt? It can be dirt. Come down. I'll show you."

BUT I WASN'T READY for this life, this talk, this love. None of it. The sad way Rita lingered like smoke in my imagination, and around the one-year anniversary of her departure, Julia entertained some artist friends from New York City, who, I think, were either moving to Seattle or had recently returned from Seattle—this before Seattle became a cliché of the alternative lifestyle. Cobain and his boys were still laboring happily in obscurity and the rest of us could only sense that some type of sea change was in the air. Being part of it, we were oblivious to all that young life bubbling up from beneath the surface, life that would eventually burst forth only to be gobbled up, repackaged and sold as a gimmick, topped with the bow of grunge, flannel, and Starbucks—a cell phone in every pocket.

"They have these coffee bars there," Julia's friend said of Seattle. "They drink so much coffee, it's kind of crazy, but I guess it's because of the rain. And the music scene is really rad. The bands have this thrashing sound, but it's not really like metal."

"What's it like?" I asked. We were in our basement kitchen, drinking wine out of some sake cups I'd brought back from Tokyo, and Julia's friend, like most of Julia's friends, was dressed in black second-hand clothing, and she was, I thought, just a little pretentious. Julia knew her from Ohio, where they both had gone to art school together.

"I'm not sure," she said. "It's hard to describe."

I laughed and shook my head and Julia shot me a look of scorn.

What I remember most about that evening was how it ended with Julia spitting in my face and how, before that, her friend had cooked us an utterly delicious dinner of potato gnocchi, feta cheese, and spinach. "This is really good cold after you come home from the bars," she'd said, and it proved true a few hours later. This was a dish I'd steal and make my own, cooking it countless times—a first meal for all my future girlfriends, and the last thing I ever cooked my father, just a couple of days before he fell on those basement steps—but when I scoffed at Julia's friend she didn't rise to the bait. She just stared me down and asked, "What do you do, Stewart?"

Now, I have to stop here and tell you this was exactly the kind of life I yearned for when I felt stuck with Rita— the company of artists, wine, good food, but all I could do that night was scorn it—and maybe it had something to do with Julia's friend's pretension, or what I perceived as pretension, or perhaps it was the undercurrent of a sexual vibe that seemed to exist between them, or maybe the fact that Julia hung her multi-colored bras over the shower rod in our teeny tiny bathroom to dry or maybe it was just that basement kitchen, which smelled of mildew and was always cold, but I think it was something deeper than all these things—this habit I had of turning away from exactly what I wanted, this inability to understand my own bruised heart.

"Oh nothing, really," I said, answering Julia's friend's question.

Julia paused with her sake cup halfway to her lips, look-ing as if I had just slapped her. We were toast. Though we didn't know it yet, we were done. We could have gone anywhere, done anything—Seattle, New York, Europe, but I was paralyzed and I want to know why. Could it be as simple as the tiny black hairs that sprouted on Julia's nipples and occasionally got stuck between my teeth when I sucked her small breasts, so unlike Rita's tits, which were ample, smooth and dreamy white? Can a life pivot on something this shallow—a hair between the teeth? Or is it deeper? The past and future just illusion. My brother's red face, my turning away from Rita, my father falling down those steps, and me, ridiculous little me, turning away from the old man and letting him die that way, ankles and wrists strapped to the bedrails, his hands covered with those enormous white safety mittens to keep him from pulling out his IVs—all the same thing. The day after her friend left, after we'd argued as her friend slept one off upstairs, I'd call the Frog and asked if they needed any help, beginning that part of my life, the part that would lead to my departure to Montana, but in that dank basement kitchen of our trinity only the moment loomed, Julia's wine cup halfway to her lips, and she looked over at me with a pleading look.

"Oh, Stewart," she said finally, slugging back her wine, trying to save us, "just tell the truth. For once in your life, tell the truth."

I am, I would like to tell Julia now, wherever she is— after all these years, I'd like to say, I'm finally telling the truth.

IN MARCH, A COUPLE of weeks before her friends visited, on one of the first real warm days, we'd set up a couple of lawn chairs atop Julia's roof so we could sip our beers and gaze out at the Walt Whitman Bridge that connected Philly to Camden, the old poet's last home. The bridge was decked out in white lights, and on the Philly side of the river, just a few blocks from Julia's studio, among the redbrick rowhomes and church steeples reaching toward the sky, stood Independence Hall, a solemn place with marble Romanesque columns lining its entrance and an engraved plaque out front. *The Declaration of Independence was signed here, a document that declared the independence of the American colonies from British rule....* It didn't seem real, and in a way, nothing did back then, except our own lives. It's what youth lacks, I guess, perspective, and though too many people have spent too much time searching for ways to remain young, what should be offered is what the young need the most, a vision that would allow them to see themselves as they really are—brushstrokes, breaths, quivers—how they dwell so near the beginning.

That night, Julia went to the edge of the studio's roof and called back to me still lounging in my chair, maybe trying to remember those first few lines of Whitman's epic poem—*I celebrate myself, and sing myself, and what I assume you shall assume.* Julia said she wanted to show me something. I was comfortable where I was, daydreaming about Whitman, my old life with Rita—the time she and I had stumbled out of a South Street bar near midnight and run past the house where Edgar Allen Poe had penned "The Raven." Nevermore. Nevermind. Oak trees dripped rain. The silent windows of the house were like a rebuke. How spooked she was, how drunk I was, and how we had stopped running only because we were laughing too hard. Part of me was still running alongside Rita, still laughing and in love, no fault lines dividing my heart like a puzzle, but I rose that night and made my way over to Julia and slung my arm across her shoulder. She wore the same denim jacket she was wearing the night I met her, and I knew we might be together forever or we could be done in a month.

Julia shrugged me off, gave me her beer, and said, "Watch this," before she took a little running start and leapt off the roof. It was only about two feet to the next building, no big thing, but I still dropped her beer in shock, the glass shattering about the same moment Julia landed on the opposite building.

"What the fuck?" I said, my heart near my balls. "Are you insane?"

She leaned back and barked out a laugh, howling at the moon.

"Your turn," she said.

"No way," I said, thinking at the same time it was only about twenty-four inches, you could almost make it with one giant step. I suspected I was years away from my own death.

"Don't be afraid," she said as gently as my mother.

I shrugged, nodded, backed up, put down my beer, and took one big breath.

"Wait," Julia said. "Watch out for that glass."

But I'd already started running, already crunched over the glass, already felt the pinch of pain in the bottom of my foot, already knew that everything was about to change.

ABOUT THE AUTHOR

Francis Davis was born and raised in Philadelphia, but has lived most of his adult life in the West. A finalist for the 2016 Katherine Anne Porter Prize in Short Fiction for this debut collection of stories, he's received fellowships from The Millay Colony for the Arts, the Ragdale Foundation, and the Vermont Studio Center. He lives with his wife and three children in Dillon, Montana, where he's an Assistant Professor of English at The University of Montana Western.

CPSIA information can be obtained
at www.ICGtesting.com
Printed in the USA
FFOW03n0835250917
40322FF